THE SEX GIRL

THE SEX GIRL

A NOVEL BY
ALICE CARBONE

A GENUINE BARNACLE BOOK
LOS ANGELES, CALIF.

THIS IS A GENUINE BARNACLE BOOK

A Barnacle Book | Rare Bird Books
453 South Spring Street, Suite 302
Los Angeles, CA 90013
rarebirdbooks.com

Set in Minion
Printed in the United States

ISBN: 978-1-940207-71-1

10 9 8 7 6 5 4 3 2 1

Publisher's Cataloging-in-Publication data

Carbone, Alice.
    The Sex Girl : A Novel / by Alice Carbone.
    pages cm
    ISBN 9781940207711

1. Drug addiction—Fiction. 2. Alcoholism—Fiction. 3. Long Beach
(Calif.)—Fiction. 4. Love—Fiction. 5. Depression—Fiction. 6.
Suicide—Fiction. 7. Music—Fiction. I. Title.

PS3603.A725 S49 2015
813.6—dc23.

In memory of my grandmother.

To my parents, for never giving up on me.

DISCLAIMER

"Beyond the river, I've seen things you'll never see."

Change

"Changes" by David Bowie

"Why did you do it, K?" Bill asked. They were still in his bed, naked, their bodies covered by dark blue sheets, made of the finest cotton she had ever touched.

"I don't know," she whispered, turning her face towards him. "Guilt, hate, shame, I guess?"

"Jesus Christ! You are beautiful," he said, walking his fingers over her tattooed spine, resting his hand where the gothic ink sunk into the lowest curve of her womanhood. "I wish they told you more often."

* * *

IT WAS A COLD day at the beginning of March and K had just landed in Los Angeles. While impatiently waiting for her black suitcase at LAX—in desperate need of a cigarette—she remembered that the last time she was in California she was just a teenager. It was back in 1985, when she spent the summer in Long Beach for a high school exchange program. Everything was still under control back then; she was almost happy. K had no idea that things could change so fast. There was something about the act of waiting in front of a circular, slow, and strident conveyor belt full of promises and an infinite number of new beginnings that made her realize how everything would show up again in front of her eyes, eventually. It was just like energy, neither created, nor destroyed; certain things belong to us, and they always will. If we are lucky—K noted on the little black notebook that she always carried in her purse, while still waiting up front for her luggage—*they transform, just like energy.*

It was 1994, a little over a month after the massive Northridge earthquake. The devastating tremor did not keep her from taking the flight across the ocean, from the land of *La Dolce Vita*, where she had been raised.

LA had suffered major damage from the earthquake, only two years after the violent April riots of 1992. Los Angeles needed some deep healing. So did K. Concrete and plaster were not enough to rebuild her weak frame and bruised bones, but if miracles really did happen, she would be the living proof of their existence.

Her long, dark, straight hair was gone. She wanted to believe that her appearance would influence her true nature, the one that she hated. But it doesn't really work like that. She just wanted to be anybody else, with a new mind and a less complicated soul.

Her nails were still painted with midnight colors. For Los Angeles, she had chosen a more elegant Night Plum by Chanel, instead of the plain black she had been using through the past eight years.

Born in January 1970 in Northern Italy, K had survived the darkness of the eighties with a melancholic hippie anima and a toe dipped in the smoky utopia of the sixties. She had never belonged to the present. She had never thought that the future was an option to seriously consider.

The past was her obsession; it haunted her at every corner. Even if K wanted to forget, those quicksilver changes in her brain, the flashbacks of her past, were becoming more and more frequent, would not let her stay in the present. Or maybe this is the lie. Maybe she needed them. Maybe without them, K did not know who she was anymore.

"How old are you baby?"—Alex, K's former lover, lit up the aluminum foil and kissed her lips with toxic smoke. This was six years earlier—"You know it's illegal, me inside you, the needle. I mean, you like my music, you get all this shit."

"I don't belong there; you are my only chance to prove it," K recited with her gloomy voice. She was not entirely sure she knew what she was talking about.

"I'm old and you are just a kid. How the fuck old are you?" He asked again, showing something that remotely resembled genuine concern, while he was so high that he barely acknowledged K's presence touching his. For five minutes, Alex pretended he truly cared.

"You are not old. I love you." Her whisper was crawling away from his knees, where she was sitting facing his deep black eyes. Slowly moving her body like a wave, to feel his desire for the prohibited become more and more impossible to hide, K took off her panties and realized, for the first time, that she had the power to control a man.

"Oh, baby…you are not crazy, don't pretend you are." His voice was carelessly violent. He was not even considering that those words were hurting her more than what he was about to do next. "You just like what I have to offer, you do like the taste of food in your mouth. I can feel your flesh and your hips in my hands. You are just from another time, or another world. You are young and so beautiful. You like danger, don't you? This will make your pain go away. Trust me. You know, baby, you should be illegal, too…"

"You are high; get your hands off my hips, Alex. Please!" She cried. Her skin felt too uncomfortable to even exist. "Just show me how you do it," she touched the signs left from the needle on his arm, chased the vapor beautifully raising full of promises from the aluminum foil he had prepared for her. Only then did she lower onto her knees, for the first time in her life.

He was hard on my tongue—K wrote in her diary—*and I knew he loved me. I didn't care about the consequences of what I was doing. I felt warm all of a sudden, and I wasn't scared anymore. My lips followed the pressure of his blood. The more his body wanted me, the more powerful I felt. And the more I let go, the more the pulse became my own rhythm, the one leading my tongue where I knew he liked it the most.*

"Your fear turns me on. You look beautiful when you are scared. You don't belong there with them." He wasn't really what people would define as literate, but he could brag a line of poetry or two when he was high. She naively mistook good quality dope for culture. "Come live here with me," he offered on a silver plate, with some fairly pure heroin from Thailand, his hand slowly adventuring between her trembling thighs. "Leave that world and move up here," he put the plastic tube in her perfect lips. That's when he burned the magic in K's green eyes.

"I know you like it, baby, and we are alone. The sky is beautiful from up here; you can see the stars and call them by name. Smoke it deep, now. I'll do the rest."

K inhaled the vapor a little deeper than before, like she was being fed holy bread. "Yes, just like that..." he whispered, "good girl, I know you like it."

"Not tonight, K," he stopped her while she was trying to reach for a condom. Warmth came. And it overwhelmed her whole body. "Tonight we are one."

"It's my first time, Alex," she begged, completely relaxed, covered by the most beautiful chemical blanket of narcotic pleasure, but very aware at the same time of the fact that she was not able to say no to him.

"Close your eyes. You know me more than you think. It won't hurt. You are going to like it even more. Just let me in."

She did.

Since that first time, since that night up in the mountains, K's life had been spent losing herself in smoky and dirty clubs beyond the city river. Feeding her heart with music and poetry, finding some private peace in old tormented books—when she was able to concentrate—and dealing with the outside world by filling up the holes with the power of any fake-love-sex she could find along the road. Every night was exactly the same. Still, it was the only option she had considered—getting high, drinking and drowning her soul away to get through the day, anesthetizing the pain and pretending she was fine.

Many times she had thought about giving up that life, but the thought of showing her true, oversensitive self scared her to death. It seemed like no one wanted her without something in return, or some illegal, dirty fun. The damaged alter ego she had created was affecting only her, while all her old friends were moving on with their lives, checking every box society required of them, K was becoming a bulimic junkie.

Giving real life a chance was too frightening. She would rather rot in her liquid golden cage, the one that she was unintentionally nailing shut and carefully refining to perfection.

Confused and overwhelmed by the riddles of life, K searched for its answers but lost herself in every dark and dirty hole she found on the way. Until the day she arrived in Los Angeles and made a U-turn. After all, she had changed her hair color, makeup, and nail polish for California; her soul would follow, eventually.

It was just like energy. It could not be destroyed.

Apologies

"The Memory Remains" by Metallica

I t was March, 1994.

Since K had arrived in Los Angeles just a few days earlier, she had been desperately trying to look perfect and professional, always according to her own idea of what people could expect of her. As she woke up at 6:00 a.m. in her hotel room, she felt that something had changed in her new life as an LA-based Italian journalist. The light breeze of early March brought her back to a deadly place where she could smell blood and cocaine, feel a body she hated, hear the voice in her head—the ancient cry for an early death.

K sat at the small, round table in the lobby of her hotel. The low-key elegance of the people around her made her feel uncomfortable. The Korean waiter at the hotel's café was friendly, but something along the dark, mosaic-patterned carpet covering the floor screamed grief and resentment. It was a feeling she did not understand in that moment, when everything was supposed to be beautiful, like in the movies.

K felt the discomfort on her skin and panic came back. Exploding chest, frozen hands, sweating. Unexpectedly, and with no apparent reason, everything she had left behind reappeared. Not even her morning French roast was able to keep her mind off it. She had thought about having breakfast in her room so she could hide from the world a little longer, but she did not have money to be ordering room service, and in the next few days K's expenses would become hard to sustain with a new apartment and, possibly, a car. She was trying to stay clean and did not have any contacts in town yet. She wanted to save as much money as possible in case of emergency; her parents could not afford to help her any longer, especially after how much she had stolen from them. Then again, since when did she start caring about food? Coffee was more than sufficient to start her day.

K had chosen that particular hotel because it was located on Wilshire Boulevard, one of the main arteries of the city, where buses were frequent enough to move around the first week. That morning, she had taken the bus to another hotel, on the Beverly Hills side of the same street, for an important press conference she had to attend. That morning she would make her first appearance in the hotel's media room, to officially represent the Italian press in the United States.

* * *

SHE BRIEFLY CHECKED THE map, managing the precarious balance of an elegant small black clutch, her cigarette, and a hot, steamy, paper coffee cup. That's how it all started; with a hot drop of coffee on her pale hand. As K dried it with a napkin, her eyes fell on the vertical, self-inflicted scar marring her right wrist. Good intentions echoed in her head like a rosary prayed in May, the month of Mary— she had genuinely planned to finally close that chapter of her life the day she moved.

"I am more than an endless list of wrong choices," she recalled saying to her doctor, the day before her flight, for a final check up and the last prescription, "I need to prove it to myself; I can do better than this."

But leaving everything behind had not been a breeze, despite what her friends thought when she had announced she would give America a try.

"Stop complaining, K," a former coworker in Italy told her over the phone, "palm trees that look like fireworks and endless summers? Are you kidding me? And you are still hanging on to that old shit, to Marco? You know K, I tried, but I've given up on you. I don't get you. Do you realize how lucky you are?"

"I never said I wasn't." K defended herself from what she perceived as another accusation. She already regretted the effort at some kind of understanding from someone she thought was a friend. "I am just saying it ain't easy."

"Be happy for Christ's sake. For once! You are in fucking California. Stop being a victim and send me a photo with a celebrity."

The thought of Hollywood Boulevard with its stars had not even crossed her mind until that moment. *Why can't I be like them?* She thought, hanging up the phone. *Everything would be so much easier if I were stupid and didn't care.*

Eight years had passed since K's struggle had begun. She could pin down the exact night her life changed forever. Closing her eyes she could remember the smells and the voices, the bitter tastes, and every weapon that had helped to bring oblivion. It was crystal clear in her mind; she couldn't help but go back and feel that moment again and again. Remembering, somehow, made her feel safe. She didn't know what could become of her if she stepped out of the shadows. The door of the past was always open, and the deadly choices always at her disposal.

Have you ever lived such an intense experience that you want to remember it forever? Recalling the smell, your heartbeat, and each word that has been said? A very early writing in her diary noted, *I keep walking back and forth through time, just to make sure I'm not leaving anything behind. Some memories I wish I could forget. But for some I need to feel a sense of belonging.*

Memories fade away when they are not supposed to, she continued, not aware that I would exist in such a near future and that I would read her words. *As of today, walking the old road is my only weapon to feel alive and worthy of breathing.*

* * *

K HAD BEGUN TO show signs of a slow and subtle collapse at the age of sixteen. She lived with her parents in an old house by the lake, on the other side of the railroad, in the cold northwest region of Italy. It was up in the Alps, in a small town close to Turin—the first capital of the country, a city that lies on the axis of white and black magic, where angels, Satan, and the Holy Shroud share the same stage, and haunt some of the most beautiful jewels of art the old country is famous for.

The neighborhood she grew up in was working class, but nice and safe nonetheless. It wasn't the best in town and yet the small park across the street from the three-story building at Number Seventeen—the one with pale yellow walls and dark green curtains on each balcony—was some kind of pure memory from her childhood, just like the whistle of the many trains heading to the French border in the early morning. She couldn't picture herself being raised anywhere else, where seasons still changed and the treasure of life was still passed down through the wrinkles of the elders. A small town, where the brand of her blue jeans was not a mandatory requirement in order to be accepted by society, where she could still drink tap water and cherish the taste of fresh snow in her mouth.

It is a mystery how K became such a tormented figure, given her apparently idyllic upbringing. Her parents were not rich, but she could honestly say that they always did their best to give her everything she needed, freedom included. It was just administered in the wrong dosage; too much for K to handle properly.

During her teens, her chain-free family life was something she was proud of, especially when every girl in school wished she had such a cool best friend for a mother who let her smoke cigarettes without hiding it.

"I'd rather you admit you smoke," her mother told K one day. "I don't want you to ever hide anything from me."

Truth was everything in the family nest.

With time, cigarette after cigarette, truth after truth, lies came easy, she confessed to her journal, not really sure that it was the cause for what she had become, but just trying to understand where it all had begun. *And the gift of freedom led me to secretly hurt myself. I was in pain. I didn't know why. I felt abandoned, I felt ugly. I felt different. No one ever noticed. No one ever heard my voice, so I stopped talking. I didn't know how to love and how to be loved in return. That gift of freedom became a double-edged sword. Of course, I wasn't aware of it at first, but I started building a new secret identity, which would shape and rule my life. I will never forget that first cigarette when learning to play guitar. I was never any good at strings, but I became a master in the art of playing with words and people.*

The beautiful mask was ready to be worn and carried around town—from the church to the nearest cemetery, not really far from where she lived. K's beautiful face was about to disappear or smile, according to what the circumstances required. She would become an on-demand dispenser of emotion.

* * *

I KNOW K'S PARENTS. They did love her. That's why I still can't understand how they let it happen. Dealing with K was daunting, but they seem to have ignored the map of visible scars on her skin. Poisoned by fear and resentment, she did eventually vomit her truth, but by then there was not much left they could do.

If it took years for her parents to realize that her thin body was dying and that her arms were bleeding, it would take her an entire lifetime to forgive them for being blind, too scared to open their eyes and admit their daughter's imperfection.

* * *

K'S FATHER WORKED IN a local photography shop, while her mother was a nurse for the small hospital a few miles north from where they all lived. They were and still are good-hearted and simple people, very naive, in a sense, and genuinely rooted in a vision of life that was slowly disappearing in those years of change.

"We wanted a daughter so much, K!" It was with agony that I read of her mother's desperate effort every time K would question the honesty of her family nest. "How can you think we do not love you?"

"So what's your complaint now, Gemma?" K argued. She had not called her Mom since early childhood. As usual, she would barely let her finish a sentence. "What's wrong with me?"

"Why can't you call me Mom?"

"Oh, come on, don't bring that up again!" K said, irritated by the same request all over again, "I never called you Mom. Do I have to show you all the old tapes from when I was four? You never had a problem with that! I've always been everything you wanted me to be. I was good in school. I did everything by myself. I never asked for your help!"

"That's why we always trusted you! We knew we didn't have to worry about you. Where did your smile go, Love?"

"Stop calling me that! Have you ever asked yourself if that perfect smile you remember was even real? Have you ever wondered if I was really happy?"

"Your lines, your cheeks, you are disappearing..." Her mother gently reached for her daughter's face.

"Oh, now you notice that I am disappearing? It's been going on for over a year, and now you are worried? What are you scared of, that men might look at me and not at you anymore? Is that because you are getting old and you don't want me to be a woman? Stop pretending that's not what it's all about," K finally said. Weak bones cracked the skin of her unwanted womanhood. Every morning in the mirror, she searched for reassurance and strength.

"You've always been beautiful. Is that why you stopped eating?"

"Oh my God! How stupid are you? Do you think that I want to walk the runway? Jesus Christ! And I thought you were going around town saying I was the smart one. That's what you think of me? Why do you keep lying to your friends about me, by the way? Does it make you shine on a podium? You know what? I am not going to discuss this with you, Gemma. Just stop talking about me. And leave me alone, okay? I'll finish high school and leave this fucking hell!"

K's father remained silent.

"Well, we are taking you to the hospital, so you will have to discuss this with someone. This game is over now."

"You will never stop this game for me." K's voice hurt them deeply. "You set me free a long time ago, now don't act like you care." She proudly showed both her parents the wounds on her left hand, the ones caused by her daily purging routine, as though they were earned in battle. "You want to pay for a private hospital? Fine, it's your choice, but this is my life and I am going to live it my way."

"You are killing yourself, K. You were so perfect!" Gemma said from deep within her heart, something that K read as pity. K's father did not move. He stood still, in complete silence.

"I've never been perfect, you made up this whole fairy tale of a perfect daughter, and you never saw how much I was hurting inside," she cried, still sitting on her bed, under which she was hiding photos of food and empty boxes of cereal for her nightly binge. "This is perfect to me," she cried again, taking off her brown sweater and showing off her skeleton ribs. "It's too late for you to notice!"

She grabbed her coat and the backpack spilled open on the floor, revealing a diary and a thick anthology of Italian literature with a red cover. She walked to the living room without looking back. She shut the door and left the house in tears.

* * *

About Love and Need

FROM THAT NIGHT, MY secret was out yet no one took it seriously enough to stop the war inside me, K wrote in LA when recalling that day in 1987. *My parents remained in agony for days not knowing where I was. But when I came back, nothing really changed. The wall between us just grew higher and thicker. And my sickly voice louder. My parents had admitted I was sick, which meant I was entitled to do whatever I wanted. I didn't have to be the perfect one anymore; I could finally deal with the pain inside by using my drugs of choice.*

It was just the beginning, and I had no idea how low it would drag me down.

I had nothing to lose, after all. Or so I thought.

What her mother said was true. K had never betrayed her parents' trust before. They had even trusted her when, at seventeen, she started dating Alex, a thirty-two-year-old dope fiend trying to get clean.

"He looks like Cary Grant. I know he is dangerous…" she always said to justify the inclinations of her early and confused taste in men, "but I know he loves me. And with me," she used to say, like a mantra, more to convince herself than to actually reassure other people, "with me, he is going to change."

Alex had possibly been an attractive man in the past, but his skin now looked bruised and heavily scabbed from years of heroin—his teeth showed signs of early decay and one was missing on the bottom left side. K was the only one in the entire world who could be attracted to such a man and she loved him to death. She gave away every penny and every inch of flesh to build their paper house on that ground of ash.

She would run away from home and threaten her parents that she would completely disappear if they ever tried to stand in her way.

I am going to be with him anyway, a note she left in their bedroom read, *with or without your approval!*

They let K follow the dangerous path of "love," though they did not like him and worried for her. They did not want to lose her, but she was already long gone.

K lost her virginity to Alex, who sang in a mediocre Jethro Tull cover band and did not care about anything but scoring his next fix. He was trying to get clean at one point, but not for K. Getting loaded was his top priority. K would find out the meaning of that need herself soon enough.

"It will make all the pain go away," Alex told her, that night up at his mountain cabin. K would never forget those words. From then on, when the pain became unbearable, she knew what to do and how to get it.

What I was doing at the very beginning, just to have fun or to keep starving myself to death, ended up becoming something I had to do to feel normal, to wake up in the morning—most of the time against my will. I lied to everyone and I was barely surviving, K wrote years later. *If you think you're smart enough to keep it under control you're just telling another lie. And I ended up becoming such a good liar! That need destroyed me in the subtlest way. I didn't care. I hated myself every day for doing it, yet I couldn't stop.*

I wasn't planning on becoming this. It wasn't my childhood dream—I wanted to be a pediatrician. But one day I didn't have a choice, I needed more and more. Whether it was a plate full of cocaine or food to throw up...I needed to hurt myself to hide the greater pain of my own breathing. I hated myself so much that I needed my brain to disappear and stop screaming inside my head. And I gave in. I gave all the way in.

The first time she gave herself to Alex was on a snowy winter night. He had rented an apartment in the woods from an old couple that farmed horses, three chickens, and a rabbit with a black spot on its left ear. The apartment was poorly furnished—he barely had the money to cover the rent—but it was rustic and made of dark oak. It looked like a warm mountain chalet to her eyes. She gave herself to him for the first time with the firm belief of saving him from his sad destiny. Instead, K fell in love, both with Alex and with the power he seemed to hold in his hands.

They did not make love. They had sex. He fucked her strung out and off in another world. She thought that was love; she built an entire existence around that idea. He became the archetype of a man for K. In her head, she did not deserve anything more than that, a part-time affection with no future and no self-respect. She became a woman overnight, without even knowing what that meant. When it was over, she drove her car back home on an icy freeway, twenty minutes south from where he lived. She was still a kid, after all, and her curfew was 11:30 p.m.

You know what's scary? she wrote in her diary, shortly after she had moved to Los Angeles. *I remember the first time I threw up like it was yesterday. I can tell you exactly what I had for dinner that night. It was zucchini squash and oven-roasted turkey. I was wearing a navy blue sweater when I knelt at that fucking toilet. You know what else, Bill? I do remember my first binge of cocaine, all night until nine the morning after. It was with an ex-boyfriend, and we were watching porn, three women. It was summer and I was drinking beer and Scotch. He hated whiskey. That's why he got himself a bottle of rum. I felt powerful and perfect, line after line, fearless, and everything was under control. I was sexy, irresistible, only covered by a black lace thong, the one he had bought for me. I know you have heard it all before, with all the women you've had. But, please, let me continue before I change my mind and go back to silence again. I can't forget any of those first times. When the hurt became too much, I had to cross the line without even considering the consequences of my actions. I never did consider them; what I could leave behind and who might get hurt along the way, the lies and the damage, the blood, and what could not be repaired. And warmth comes, eventually, so overwhelmingly beautiful that I liked the needle even more than sex. Do you remember how pain would fade away and everything would slow down with your heartbeat? You know what I'm talking about, because you are the only one who can truly understand. And, I know you won't judge me. You care for me.*

The scary thing in all of this, K wrote, *is that I don't remember the first time I had sex. I completely removed that night from my memory. I have a clear image of him in my head. Actually, I still have his photo in my wallet. I know I did what he told me to do. But don't ask me if there were candles or music playing. I don't remember how I felt afterward. We were smoking and I was half naked. I took off my panties, and I remember being warm. I was relaxed and everything else disappeared. I was on the floor, on my knees. And, all of a sudden, it's complete darkness in my head. I can't see his bed and I barely remember what his bedroom looked like. He had black eyes and black hair, but that's pretty much it. Did I bleed? I have no idea. I don't know if it hurt or if I liked it. I didn't want to get pregnant or get HIV, but I recall we weren't safe. He didn't want to use a condom and he had Hepatitis B.*

That was the most terrifying part for me. Sometimes I even wonder if I imagined it, or if it was real. That's the scary thing, Bill. I don't know what's in my head anymore.

That's how love works. I'll be smart, she reassured herself. *I will never become like him. I'll know when to stop. I will not walk that line.*

Those were her last sober words for the next eight years.

K and her older "boyfriend" spent their time in his tiny, poorly furnished bedroom. Bloody needles and burned silver spoons (the good ones his mother gave him to start a new life after rehab), a couple of CDs were randomly piled up on an old table. The Rolling Stones,

Enya, Jethro Tull, and Patsy Cline. There was a fireplace next to the small window facing the mountain, a touch of natural warmth hard to find otherwise.

She was in love with a liar and a thief, a man who taught her all the tricks and all the rules to become just like him. Not really for the drugs, but for the ability to find an easy escape with any tool at her disposal. After almost three years she found out he was about to have a kid with another woman, already married with three daughters. That same year K graduated from high school.

"It's just high school, K." The therapist tried to explain the day she had agreed on talking to a professional for the first time. More so to prove to her parents that truly there was something wrong with her than to actually try and fix anything. "We all went through high school. Why do you feel it's different for you? Why do you think your parents sent you here?"

"I should be honest with you, since they are paying for this, right? Well…" K continued, "for as much as I love them, they have no idea who I am. Do you want to know the only time I feel heard? It's when I'm with Alex."

"K, I talked to your parents about it. His world is heroin. And he is too old for you." K noted the doctor's antiseptic pronunciation of the word heroin. It made her wonder why the old woman had chosen that professional path, if drugs shocked and disgusted her so much. "You didn't do that, did you?" Dr. Daniela said, with her carefully redesigned lips that looked like they belonged in an old postcard from the forties. She adjusted her tweed skirt on the expensive leather of the chair. The studio was in a beautiful baroque building in downtown Turin and the cream-colored stucco of the façade almost blended with the sky and the city lights, at sunset.

"Listen, I had to take a train and two buses to get here and see you, do you think I did heroin?"

"Don't answer my questions with another question, K."

"I did not do heroin," she lied, outraged by such an insinuation. "The point is that I'm invisible to them. They think I make up things just to be different, to be special, and to be at the center of attention."

"Who are you talking about?"

"My classmates. They can't see the pain; they don't understand why I hurt or my relationship with Alex. They think these wounds…" she said, showing her arms, "is me, begging for a spotlight. I was fat the first year of high school. I will never forget their eyes on me on my first day when I walked in. I will always remember what I was wearing and the way they treated me, how they laughed." Being a late addition to Class B, K was introduced by the principal himself to a full class of young students who were already bonding and making plans on where to get coffee during the ten o'clock fifteen-minute break.

"They think I make things up, even the fact that he loves me. Just because I don't like their fucking music and I don't dress like they do. And they end up copying me, by the way!" K continued, proudly owning her sick-thin body—a work in progress.

"I am sure they will find someone else to torture, sooner or later. There's a new girl already, with braces and big lips; she will probably take my place, eventually. But they still don't know what it's like. They don't go beyond body fat, braces, thick glasses, and pimples; they're just bullies."

"You are a little bit too sensitive," the doctor said dismissively. "It's honestly too early to diagnose any form of depression or a real eating disorder for that matter. You know what I mean? You lost what? Fifteen pounds, maybe?" The doctor smiled, ready to close the session and get the eighty bucks for the hour. "I can prescribe a mild therapy with Prozac, if that makes you feel better. But I would wait to officially diagnose you with real depression. You are too young to be depressed. Prozac won't hurt you." She handed her patient the prescription.

"Thank you, but I am not done here. Prozac won't really listen to what I have to say." K put the prescription in her purse thinking that, finally, she did not have to steal her grandmother's sleeping pills anymore. She looked outside. It had just stopped snowing. Turin looked beautifully placid. Everything was covered in white. Not many cars were on the usually very busy streets. And it seemed like the few buses that were still in service tried not to disturb their private, yet deluded conversation.

"They either laugh at me or they call me a whore. I never tried to steal their boyfriends. I can't even look at myself in the mirror, how do you think I can be interested in stealing their boyfriend? I don't care! I am in love with Alex. Can you at least trust me? I just want to be left alone.

I'm not really interested in their stupid world. I wish they would just understand! I need silence! This isn't just high school. Could you please believe me? How much weight do I have to lose for you to trust me? Can I smoke, please?" The way K assumed she could do whatever she wanted was astonishing even to a psychiatrist who had seen it all before.

"You are barely eighteen, dear," Dr. Daniela politely denied.

"My mother lets me smoke whenever I want to."

"Well, you will have to wait until we're done here." She dismissed K's request. "Tell me something now; your mother tells me you talk about death. Would you explain why?"

"I don't want to live like this."

Death was something that had always occupied K's mind. Just like getting married and having kids did for many young girls her age. She had always fantasized about being old and ready to die, like her grandmother. She could vividly see herself with her wrinkled face. Ivory powder to protect her skin and make her beautiful. She could smell homemade strawberry preserves for breakfast, hear a Mahler LP scratching from time to time. Asleep at sunset, just to wake up at dawn and start the simple routine again up in the mountains by the frozen river, waiting by the kitchen window for the final call to take her somewhere else, where peace was supposed to reign over the resting souls.

She was taken with Leonard Cohen, not with the popular pop bands or with the hot soccer player of the national team. He was the ultimate poet. He made her feel embraced and less alone. He wrote about the same despair she felt and made it come alive on a guitar string. His humble handsomeness was irresistible. In him, she had finally found someone different, but in the real world, she was still lonely. K was someone that people loved to be around fifty percent of the time, and loved to hate the other fifty percent.

Maybe that old doctor was right. It was just high school. But what every teenager feels in those crucial years of growing up became K's excuse to handle and manipulate people and life. It became her role, the perfect victim, so that she could blame someone else for her own misery.

It's December again, I read in the diary, from when K was eighteen, *and like every year, I am waiting for Christmas. I always have the highest expectations for that day. However, when December twenty-fifth comes, I end up disappointed. I wonder if all the people experience this feeling, the hope for something new, for not belonging to the day that is.*

Why do they make us dream of something so intensely if the outcome, the real deal, is bitter and dreary to taste, not remotely close to what the commercials broadcast?

You know, I let that feeling of warmth and perfection penetrate me so much that the moment I realize that it is something impossible to attain, I lose everything, every fiber of strength to believe again. You might think I am making a big deal out of nothing—it's just Christmas, after all. But that's why I find myself here, on a Friday night. Alex is probably on some sidewalk waiting for his dealer to show up. I'm dry. He forgot we were supposed to have dinner.

All my other friends are having Irish coffee at Eleanor's birthday party. I feel uncomfortable around people. That's why I didn't go. I am not like them. I get lost in stupid details that are of secondary importance. I don't fit in with the way they talk.

With time, I am getting to understand that this very innocent habit of mine is often misunderstood for weirdness; they run away from it.

Grandma, too, writes a diary every night before going to sleep. After she has washed the dishes, and watched Derrik, *her favorite German police TV show. Sometimes she writes what she did with Grandpa during the day, or the groceries they have bought, the dinner she has made, or how many Lorazepam she had to take in order to get by and make it to 9:00 p.m. without killing herself.*

Why does it really matter what kind of details I am drawn to? These are the things that give me a sense of belonging. I want to be buried next to Grandma when I die. I have already told Gemma and Dad.

I went to a therapist for the first time. But she said there's nothing wrong with me.

I didn't binge and didn't throw up today. I just smoked some pot. I didn't take any real drugs. I can't really think straight, I can't sleep, and I don't know where to find Alex.

The doctor said I am not depressed. But she gave me some pills, just in case. You know how they are: the more the better. Or, at least this is what they do with Grandma. She can't live without pills anymore. But she is still so beautiful with her silk scarf and her bouclé coat. She is always elegant, sublime, even when she cries. Maybe pills do really work for people like us.

K's grandmother Silvia died a couple of days after K's graduation, in the town's small hospital in the hills.

"Be good, Love," Silvia said before she passed away. K was the last person to talk to her in the hospital room. "I'll keep an eye on you."

Right after kissing her for the last time, K got on a plane to London. She didn't attend the funeral.

It was the end of July, 1989.

Everything was supposed to happen in the rainy and royal land, but nothing actually did. With a guitar and a suitcase full of promises, K got deeper into drugs, lies, and debts, just a few blocks from the Notting Hill Gate tube station. The memory of the violent crises with her loved and hated father never faded.

How could she forget the first time she ran away from home when she was seventeen years old? She was hiding behind her obsession with Alex, but on a deeper level she was trying to escape the constant judgment and the exhausting fights with a father whose ideas she could not accept anymore. She needed to hurt him to prove to herself that she could grow different—immune to his quick-tempered nature. The truth was that something had gone wrong, so K could not bear intimacy with him, though she desperately needed his love and acceptance.

She tried very hard to change for her father. She practically killed herself, starving and intoxicating her body. She became the opposite of what she was inside, in search of love and her true self.

Very soon I started to believe in each and every one of his words. "You are not my daughter anymore. You will never learn how to live, so ungrateful for what you have!"

I did not want to be his daughter. Maybe, I did not even deserve a father and I was better off that way, K wrote. *There were days when he was proud of me though, when I delivered something extraordinary, that he couldn't help but notice. I was his daughter, after all. When I graduated from college, after discussing my thesis on the JFK Assassination, I had red roses in my hands, proud friends and family by my side; I still can't believe he didn't want to be there.*

"If you miss this celebration," Gemma told my father the day before the ceremony he had no intention of attending, *"you are gonna regret it forever. She is your daughter. Don't be stupid."*

Sick and still blind to her condition, K had barely made it through college. She graduated with decent grades, while slowly sinking, flirting with oblivion by means of any possible drug and daylight drunkenness. She had not given her best, but thinner than ever, she kept achieving the goals she was supposed to reach—those she felt were expected of her, in order to be socially acceptable.

"Why can't you pick a side and stick to it, once and for all?" she argued with her mother. "Either you are with me or with Dad."

"I love you both. Just apologize to him and everything is going to be fine." Gemma's begging was painful yet so tender that it wasn't my place to judge why she did it. "I want peace in this family, don't you get it? I'm just trying to help."

"You won't have peace. Where's your loyalty, for Christ's sake? Stop defending me in front of him just to blame me a couple of hours later when we are alone! What kind of lesson are you teaching me? Apologizing for what? It's all about apologies for you, even when I didn't do anything wrong. I don't have to save my marriage like you do, Gemma. I am not married to him!" Rage flared up like lava from her mouth. "That's your choice and you shouldn't put me in the middle of it. It isn't fair!" Her words went unheard, that day like on many others, when K tried to tell Gemma her truth.

But Gemma's priority at that point wasn't K's peace of mind. Her marriage, and the family balance was. The lesson she taught K was a dangerous one: If you apologize, everything is going to be fine.

"You two just need to talk K…"

"No, you just need to mind your own business. I only apologize when I make a mistake. There's nothing to save here."

Hurting Gemma was just another way to hurt herself—her mother's tears just more salt on her wounds. K felt powerless; hurting those who loved her made her feel in control. She did not want to hurt her mother. She just wanted Gemma to understand what a big mistake she was making. Nevertheless, K ended up spewing rage and frustration on her, never resolving the real conflict. Gemma's door was shut to any kind of conversation that might jeopardize the safety of her relationship with her husband. When K finally understood that, she just gave up.

Gemma had just become the perfect target, to the extent that K began to doubt her own humanity. She was able to give such emotional cruelty and hate toward the woman, and somehow it gave her new life, energy, and pride.

The first time K talked thoroughly about the relationship with her father was years later, when she had already settled in Southern California.

"Can you believe my father never waited up for me at night when I was out with friends?" K asked her friend Dawn over coffee. She sipped from the orange teacup, dreaming it was codeine cough syrup. "I would come home late and completely fucked up, and he would be asleep in his bed. Was your father asleep when you were shooting dope, up in San Francisco? I am sure he was not. He was worried for you."

"This is good, K. Let it out. "

"I craved his attention like I craved dope. I longed for his attention like a binge, like a cut. I needed it when I was younger, but he was asleep—not even on the couch."

She was facing the truth for the first time, written down in columns, when trying to justify the resentment and the rage she had never thrown back at him, but heaped on herself, with no mercy whatsoever.

For a long time K had dismissed those feelings. They were not enough to be classified by the general public as a degraded background or a painful childhood experience that could lead a little girl to suffer deeply and eventually dig her own grave. She hated her parents' pride in front of the church community. They just bragged about their family, nothing but perfect. To her eyes, it was all lies. And she never had the courage to talk about it with anyone until Bill.

"She is so mature for her age, you are so lucky!" Friends and church members would compliment Gemma and Aldo, my dad, during the weekly family meetings. "You know guys," the butcher would then step in, standing up proud like the minister of the holy music on the podium, with dark red traces of blood under his fingernails, leftovers from an ordinary day of work, "You stand as an example here, your family I mean. You should give a talk sometime. Have you ever thought about leading the meeting with a topic every week?"

The old church that stands just across the railroad is where both my parents and grandparents have had most of their friends and social community life. Every Wednesday night they meet in the small room, the one with the red carpet, where the choir rehearses on Thursday. They just share their struggles and challenges in raising their kids, keeping the marriage alive, and all other sorts of issues. Bullshit! They keep lying to each other and they have no idea of what happens behind closed doors. They have no clue that the perfect family has a far-from-perfect daughter.

I just wish they would stop pretending for Christ's sake!

If everything was so perfect, why would she ever be depressed and in such suffocating despair? The same way that depression wasn't contemplated and accepted for her grandmother, it wasn't for K either.

"Why don't you stop pretending you are like her already?" Aldo kept asking K. "You are going to end up dead sooner or later if you don't cut it out."

"Why can't you accept that I am sick?" Her tearful scream would echo in the kitchen, where most of their fights would take place. She would then leave her dinner untouched, if not for some crumbles of Southern bread on the red tablecloth.

"Because you are not! You are a lucky one. We shouldn't have spoiled you so much with all your bullshit!" He yelled, while K headed toward her bedroom. "Yeah, right, keep running away. That's the only thing you know how to do; you hide in your bedroom. You are not like her! Stop faking it. After all we have done for you. It's unbelievable. I am tired of you!"

The more she would try to justify and explain her condition, later in her young womanhood, the more they failed to understand. Still, they couldn't help but feel guilty.

"What have we done wrong? You have always been free," her mother said as she ironed bedsheets in the kitchen.

"Why do you iron bed sheets anyway? Can't you just enjoy a winter afternoon?" K tried to avoid the uncomfortable conversation, almost like she knew where it was headed.

"Don't change the subject, K! I'm serious. Stop pretending you know what's best for me and show some respect! You don't know anything about relationships, and you don't know anything about my marriage."

"What do you want to know then? Isn't my being sick enough?"

"I want to know where it comes from. Do you remember how much I have sacrificed for you, even when your father was against it? Do you remember all those late nights downtown when you were fourteen and wanted to be a singer? That album you recorded in Turin, with people three times your age? I would pick you up at two in the morning on a school night, while normal teenagers were in bed. Wouldn't you call that love?"

"Was it, Gemma? Or were you just so afraid I would run away and do things by myself? Or, even worse, hate you? Were you afraid I would blame you for not even trying to help me make my dreams come true?"

"Dreams? Please be serious." She allowed the words to freely flow, while cleaning up the ashes on the table and emptying the ashtray, without even thinking about the implications of what she was about to say. "You live in your dreams. You can't even fit in something that isn't bigger or better, unattainable. Grow up K! You are not a child any more."

"I was a grown-up at three, Gemma. And you were all very clear and very proud of that. Don't you remember? Too busy taking care of poor Alessio that couldn't even speak and ask for a glass of water?"

"Cut it out, K. Don't bring up your brother again! Why do you want to hurt me?" The kitchen never felt as emotional as that afternoon. The bitter cold of a way-too-early winter felt warmer than the frozen nest inside. "We loved you and we wanted you from the very first day. Do you have any idea how much we dreamed of having a daughter? We gave you everything, and we were just going along with what we thought you needed. Every time you wanted to try something new, we were there for you. You tried to be a model in Milan and we spent money we didn't have to make that happen, to take those beautiful photos of you."

"See what you are doing again?" K screamed. Her face turned red with rage. She lit another cigarette and filled up her glass with water to swallow the increasing number of Xanax she was taking every day. She avoided Gemma's eyes and continued to talk. "I am trying to tell you what I feel, and you hold against me the list of all the amazing things you did? Can you try and listen for once? I haven't even blamed you for my pain and you already feel guilty."

"Is that what you are trying to do? Blame me? Because that's unfair, K." Gemma replied, now putting down the iron and walking towards the terrace. She closed the window that K had opened to let some of the smoke out.

"Gemma, please," K said, her voice tired of arguing. "I can't talk about this."

"No, now you listen. If I have to be blamed along with your father for your failures, will you at least shut up and listen to me!

"Do you remember how we allowed you to date Alex? He was old and a drug addict, yet you seemed so in love! Did we prevent you from having that affair?"

"It was not an affair!"

"That's not the point. Don't play with my words like you always do. We did not. We thought you should explore your feelings and now you have become just like him. We believed in you."

"What did you believe, Gemma? That I could save the life of an old junkie? Because that's what I believed!" K yelled, almost out of breath and now clenching her fists.

"Let me finish, K! You look just like your father! I didn't want your lies, so I let you be yourself. Do you realize you are free to smoke in front of me?" Gemma asked, not mentioning those pills. Gemma wasn't aware of all the drugs K was taking at the time.

"Yes, let's talk about that! You would rather have my honesty; and God knows how much I loved the day you told me cigarettes would kill me yet you didn't want me to hide anything from you. How the hell did you think it would do me any good?"

"I just wanted to be your best friend."

"I wanted that, too. That's why I never called you Mom. But I needed a mother first!"

Their dialogue was heartbreaking to take in, when Bill first gave me K's diary. However, I could not stop digging into the truths of her life. It was not easy to put all those fragments together in an authentic and respectful way, without compromising what had truly happened.

"Can I write about her freely?" I asked Bill one day, after he had revealed those old pages of hers.

"Are you sure you really want to go into that, Angie?" He replied with distance and sincere concern at the same time. "I thought you deserved to know, that's why I am giving this to you, but you won't always like what you are going to read." He finished his tea and went back to the kitchen table where we were having breakfast.

"Have you ever read it all?" I asked. I wasn't hungry any more. I gazed at Manhattan through the frozen window to avoid the sadness in his eyes.

"I have read some of it. But I didn't have to read it all. I know what happened. I lived with her and she confessed everything."

Bill kissed and tenderly caressed my hair. He put on a navy sweater and left the room, intentionally leaving the diary on the table. That day, I made sure no trace of coffee or morning food had stained the old black book. I finished what was left of my breakfast and went to my room holding the diary in my hands. I didn't read it that day; I wasn't ready. I decided I would keep it safe until the perfect night. I had to find out who she really was. I had to make sure the time was right to enter K's world. That's how this story started. Writing a book about it was merely a coincidence, a tribute I owed to her tormented soul. It was the only way to finally set her free and close a chapter—for me—that had remained opened for too long.

K changed many therapists over the years. But it was only with Dr. Carmen, just one year before her big move to Los Angeles, that she felt heard for the very first time.

"They love me, I know, but they never saw me. I consciously made every decision—whether it was throwing up, or drugs, or cutting myself. I don't want to hurt them." K felt ashamed of her twisted feelings towards her parents. "But they are responsible, too. Don't tell me the fault is all mine. It wasn't high school. They knew what I was doing, maybe not always, but they knew when I was ten years old. I never told anyone, it's just too sick."

"What happened when you were ten?"

"I can't believe I am sharing this," her voice more embarrassed than ever. "I don't even know how it started, but I had a habit back then, before I even knew there was something wrong with me—Jesus, this is hard!"

She walked to the window in order to avoid the doctor's eyes, and therefore talk more freely. The day was a sunny one. Kids played in the small park across the street from the doctor's office. She closed the curtains not to be distracted. Yet she did not turn her head to face Dr. Carmen.

"I would cut my big toe nail, and would get it infected. I mean," she explained, to be more clear about the surgical procedure she would obsessively perform on her body when still a child, "repeatedly, for years, and every time the infection would heal, I would do it again, and again, and again. My mom knew. She was the one constantly buying antibiotic cream. Why didn't she ask what was going on? Wouldn't you wonder what's wrong with your daughter who has her foot infected five times a month for years?"

"Why did you do it?" Dr. Carmen asked, not shocked at all by K's confession.

"I found pleasure in it. In the pain, and in the danger that the infection wouldn't heal, I could see where I stood. The pulsating pain of the infected flesh made me feel something that I wasn't feeling otherwise. I felt in control of it. It gave me power. I could stop it and decide when I wanted it again. I was only ten. And they never asked themselves what was wrong with their daughter. Now, tell me: I was a kid then, don't you think that maybe I could have been saved?"

"Can you see a pattern here?" Dr. Carmen said, "Don't take this the wrong way, I am just trying to help you, but can you see the position you keep putting yourself into?"

"Yes. And, I am always the one who gets hurt."

"You need to be the one who gets hurt. You are getting something out of it; that's the pattern. Would you say that? I don't want an answer. I just want you to sleep on it, when you are on your own. You are a young woman now. It's only up to you. You are the only one who can end this war."

Three

"Chloe Dancer/Crown of Thorns" by Mother Love Bone

K's struggle with eating disorders had started— by choice at first—at the age of sixteen on a regular, boring day of school and the homework that followed. After a couple of hours studying, K decided to take a break from the essay she was writing on Lord Byron. She hurried into the seventies-style kitchen, made of brown and metallic finishing, with a white round table in the middle and a futuristic black crystal lamp. She made some tea and passed by a jar of biscotti on the shelf. She ate one. K was tired of being alone that afternoon. She could not stand her heavy body anymore. That is why she decided to call her friend Sarah or, as K called her in her diary, the blonde dead-girl, who, for the first time, even before her junkie boyfriend, introduced K to a new life path.

Sarah was K's nearest neighbor. She was three years older than her, and lived across the street from Number 17. They were both taking a break from homework. After a short catch up on the phone, they decided to meet at the local park, the one with the old rusty teeter-totter and a broken slide. With nothing but a boxed apple juice and a stolen cigarette, K waited for Sarah on the south bench, the green one, under the weeping willow. It almost felt like she already knew her life was about to change. It almost felt like the big revelation was about to be written down in blood.

"You won't be able to even eat a piece of chocolate," Sarah told her. "Guilt is going to haunt you. You'll wish nothing but sleep, but you won't be able to."

"What do you mean?" K asked, clueless of what anorexia really was.

"I can't sleep, K. I wish I could get some rest from the voice in my head. But I just can't. I dream about food all the time. That's the down part of it." Sarah explained almost like she was describing some kind of esoteric practice. "I cut every picture of food from my mom's magazines. And those photos fill me up a little, although it doesn't last long. This is hardcore, K. It's not a diet; it's going to be your new life. This body has a price." She finished her lecture, touching her hipbones and having no clue of what her body truly looked like to a healthy human being.

Sarah was all skin and bones. And K had envied her body and ethereal beauty for quite a long time. She had always wanted to be like her. Sarah looked powerful and self-confident. A popular singer in town even wrote a song for her, a love song. Sarah was so strong and determined that K felt of secondary importance, to the point where she decided to ask for her friend's help. It was late spring, the day was warm and Sarah wore a hippie, silky, and long emerald green dress, which perfectly matched her watery eyes. The light shined around her, creating a haunting aura. It emanated an avalanche of luminosity that would have blinded anyone looking in their direction. In that moment, K knew she was ready to undergo anything it took in order to gain that kind of power.

They talked for hours. Sarah shared with K the most dangerous secret she could ever reveal to someone. She taught K the powerful trick of how to control life. How to wear the mask no human being could ever defeat, how to control your heart and your soul, by protecting them from the external world with a magic potion, a deadly drug.

K would plan her whole life based on that confession. It would become her best friend and her worst enemy, her strength and her weakness, her weapon and her own poison. That secret would become the voice in her head.

The same night, once back home, K decided to slowly die; that same night, she decided she would painfully disappear, to sell her blood, to sell her soul, and to wreck her heart and her body.

Years later, K remembered every small detail of that event, like her mother serving zucchini squash and oven roasted turkey when she returned from the park. That night, for the very first time, K silently discovered her safe shelter, deep down in the small corner bathroom of the family apartment, on the seventies black-and-white floor that her knees touched for the very first time, almost with pride. She did not cry. She had never felt more powerful.

Back then K did not realize that she had just made a deal that would haunt her forever. The moment she finally understood, it would be too late. Her Los Angeles diaries opened up the door to every secret of hers. I now follow her steps to lead you there and finally free her soul. I owe this to K. I will tell you the story with her own words, those of a talented writer who fell in love, with a man and her own life.

What Sarah had just given K was, in a way, a mask to conceal the feeling of life and self.

A Brand New Start

"Country Feedback" by R.E.M.

It was March 3, 1994.

K waited fifteen minutes for the bus that would take her to the press conference. Los Angeles is not exactly a place to adventure without a car, but on that early morning, she didn't worry about how long she had to wait on the street. She had plenty of time to get to the location in Beverly Hills, retouch her makeup, and maybe even grab a cup of coffee in the refreshment room before the interview was scheduled to start. The more time she had to breathe in the new surroundings, the better she would fit in the long run. The golden warmth of Los Angeles seemed to be smiling at her. The sun was high in the sky and Wilshire Boulevard looked like a movie set.

Kissed by the vernal morning light she wished she was able to just be in the moment. K hadn't entirely surrendered to the quicksilver changes in her mind, and she knew that she had to deal with her inability to stop the near-constant flashbacks to her former life.

She needed to rehearse the Q&A to soften her Italian accent. She needed to reread the bio of the writer she had to interview one more time. But all she could concentrate on was her luggage by the door. She was scheduled to check out of the Wilshire Hotel in Koreatown by 8:00 a.m. K had reserved room number 724 just for the first week in town and, she was scheduled to move into a two-bedroom apartment with Carrie, her future roommate.

The nights spent in the hotel went smoother than she thought. No insomnia disturbed her precious and rare sleep. Jet lag and exhaustion from long days of work helped K sleep without too many pills. She hoped it would continue forever.

The *forever* issue bothered and fascinated K at the same time. She was wild and could never accept chains out of a bedroom. Nonetheless, there was a part of her personality that always looked for a forever of some kind. She always hoped for the forever to fix her life, or to simply give her some stability that—as much as she hated it—was the only weapon she could count on to stay away from danger.

"You are different," Gemma told her one night, while K was smoking a cigarette on the front porch. No matter that the conflict was bound to start again, during those rare quietudes, the two would try and have some kind of honest conversation.

"I get it. You are not like your friends. Settling down will kill you," Gemma said, while handing her daughter a cup of tea. She was almost afraid of making a mistake, like getting the wrong blend, or not properly boiling the water, would ruin any semblance of a relationship they had.

"I know, but I need it," K argued.

"You don't. It doesn't work for you. Do you want to get married, have three kids, and live two blocks from here? Do you really think it will make you happy?"

"It would save me."

"You're wild. I never know how to talk to you," she admitted, sitting down on the wooden chair next to K. "I never know how you are going to react. But do you think I never wished you were like them?"

"It hurts."

"I know it does. But everything hurts. Just stop chasing something you will never have and trust yourself..."

Deep inside K knew her mother was right.

"Do I have to remind you what all your efforts to settle down turned out to be? You became a prisoner."

"I feel like a prisoner anyway."

"Yes, but it's your choice now. Every time you fail in settling with something or someone, you fall. I don't want to get into this right now, but I see the way you eat, K. And God knows what you do when you are not here."

"It wasn't just high school."

"What went wrong?"

"I don't know. But it never went away. It's still here."

Like waking up from a deep sleep, she found herself in the hotel room again. Those first nights had gone well. She ate dinner every evening at 8:00 p.m. at the same sushi place across the street, around the corner from Normandie Ave. The spicy tuna salad had become her go-to, together with some Radiohead on the stereo. The song "Creep" was her favorite to listen to while closing her eyes and feeling less alone. But after 168 hours of safety from the outside world, she knew that she had to walk into that life she had planned when still agonizing in a single bed, wet with her cocaine and Xanax sweat of guilt and shame.

She did not leave Turin to follow a big dream, like many people had thought. K was desperate. She had been giving herself away for drunken orgasms and immediate relief. She recalled the feeling of their hands inside her body with regret, but barely remembered their names.

I did it in the cemetery parking lot and I woke up with bruises on my arms. I don't remember how, she wrote in her diary. *And, in that park downtown, of course, with Marco. I remember the old asylum turned into a bar and the empty streets, the snow, so many apartments, and a cheap motel, too. He paid for dinner, cocaine, and expensive wine after years apart. I hated myself for even going with him. I had made the wrong choice, again. I just wanted to get loaded. I needed to punish and humiliate myself with someone that I would have just rejected in a sober daylight. I didn't stop fucking him until my nose bled and my heart gave signs of cardiac arrest. I wanted to die that morning. Only then, at 10:00 a.m., did I leave the room and walk to my car. I was barely dressed, even though it was winter. I looked cheap, like a hooker in a small town. My fishnets torn with holes and everyone knew who I was, even with my sunglasses on. Ashamed, I ran away to get more drugs that would calm me down and put me to sleep. No matter how many men I could sleep with, I could never fill the emptiness inside. The morning after I just wanted to forget what I had done.*

The first morning at the new apartment turned out to be worse than she had thought. The old building they had just moved into was at the end of Bedford Street, hidden in the run-down part of the Beverlywood neighborhood of Los Angeles, between South La Cienega and Robertson Boulevards, just outside of what she thought was the corny elegance of Beverly Hills. She had found the room through local friends, when she was still in Italy.

When K woke up in her silky burgundy sheets, she felt like she was in the wrong place again. She loved being alone, but only when it was her choice, or when she was so high she couldn't even bring herself to go out and get milk.

Those were the days when she was so sick that the idea of being seen in public, without a bathroom within a few feet, was so terrifying that she simply locked herself in. Being alone with her screaming head was unbearable. Food had helped her squelch the screaming, but in her starving condition, drugs maintained her, leaving her with some sense of belonging to this damaged world of those forgotten by God. The emptiness in her body and getting loaded were the only ways to live without strain, free from her own mind.

"They became my weapon to avoid the discomfort of life, the fear, and the suffocating sense of inadequacy for my own body, for my very own breathing.

"I didn't know how it worked. But it did. And I liked it, more and more. When I didn't like it anymore, it was too late," she told Bill.

Despite the warm light of the city, Los Angeles felt foreign and empty. The new environment she was looking forward to exploring and hanging on to was not exactly what she expected it to be. Carrie was kind and sweet, but her presence did not seem to help. Back then, K had trouble seeing what she had in front of her. Carrie's bubbly, positive energy scared her to death.

When she finished moving all of her suitcases into the small room with dirty carpet and a broken, nasty bed that the previous tenant sold to her for eighty-five dollars, Carrie took her to a party downtown, to introduce "The Italian" to her friends. She did not want to go at first. She was tired and in desperate need of some peace. But Carrie was so polite inviting her along, K decided to change her pattern for one night. She ended up enjoying an all-girl night of cake frosting and pizza. She did not *eat* any of that of course (not that night, at least, since there wasn't a convenient bathroom at her disposal to get rid of the guilty food).

She ate it days later, when the leftovers of the cake in the shape of a gray seal were resting in the fridge. It made her vomit sweet and greasy gray Betty Crocker cream cheese frosting for days. But just being at the party for a couple of hours let the self-loathing cloud clear up for a little while.

"Dig, Lazarus, Dig!" by Nick Cave

"MISS?" THE WAITER CALLED, handing K a glass of iced tea at the counter. He touched her arm lightly, almost afraid of hurting her, just like you would be when trying to wake up a sleepwalker. "Your order will be ready shortly. You okay?"

"Oh, yeah, I'm sorry," K replied, embarrassed. "Jet lag," she lied, having being in town for now over two weeks.

"Is there anything else I can help you with?"

"No, that'll do it. Thanks."

"I hear an accent, where are you from?" The waiter forced the conversation.

"I'm Italian," K replied, politely, but visibly bothered by the unwanted courtesy chat.

"Oh my God! I always wanted to go to Rome. Our chef is Italian, too. You should meet him."

K hated when at the sound of the word "Italy," people told her all about their dreams of traveling to Rome or Florence. Not because she did not like those cities, but because she thought it was an ignorant cliché, which not only showed a very limited geographical culture, but was also a very superficial topic to use to start a conversation about a foreign country. Just like it would be for a French-born person raised in Provence, who wouldn't necessarily give a damn about Paris.

"Oh, cool, you should definitely visit. It's beautiful there!" She cut him off, perfectly aware of who the chef was and where he was from: Sardinia.

Mauro's Café was a newly opened little Italian restaurant in the heart of West Hollywood, on

Melrose Avenue. She chose the place because she knew the owner. And because it sounded like the perfect place to ride out her homesickness, at least with tastes and flavors, colors and sounds. The restaurant had recently become the ultimate celebrity spot that international editors loved to feature in their Spring/Summer issue, the perfect retreat for a trendy combination of quality Italian food and very expensive designer shopping.

The air smelled like white sand beaches, she recalled, thinking about the many summers spent in Sardinia, a small island in the South of Italy. *Where the sea is a blue emerald surface, heaven on earth, sunk into the wild green of the untouched soil surrounding the harbor. It's the land of white wine and sea urchins, lemons and coconut tanning oil.*

The floor of Mauro's was a raw mosaic of stones and the white walls were decorated with black and white old Hollywood photographs from the fifties. The restaurant sparkled with a golden glow and felt like a fresh breeze on my skin. I could smell pure lemon essence, Coco Mademoiselle, and watermelon.

K walked in feeling shy and inappropriate. While she waited at the counter, now on her fourth chardonnay, the long-haired rocker sitting next to her didn't take his eyes off her and seemed not to notice her discomfort.

How is it possible? she thought. It was hard to believe in Hollywood, the land of beautiful women, tall, curvy, sexy and Barbie-like bombshells, Botox's best friends, the land of eternal youth. K did not resemble that at all. Yet everyone seemed to be somehow so attracted to this tiny creature from very far away. Even the blond fifty-something guitar player that approached her at the counter while she silently waited for another drink and a lunch of egg whites with fresh baby spinach leaves. She wrote something on her black notebook, not really eager to engage in a below average pick-up conversation.

The fact that K was very shy and uncomfortable around people had always been misunderstood for rudeness and above average self-confidence. That's why most of the men who tried to approach her would quickly abandon their pursuit, and that's also why the ones who did not had a very good chance of becoming K's prey. This wasn't the case with the musician. The long-haired man quickly understood she was too complicated for an easy catch and shortly left the scene, leaving K free to keep wandering through time.

Deep Red

You will never stop it,
It will go deeper and deeper
You'll feel better and better
Deeper and deeper...
It's not your skin making me cry
It's not your touch
It's mine, my private moment
It will keep going forever and ever, 'till the end
'Till the last one,
Beyond your expectations
Beyond your darkest desires

It will get deep red, it will make you hurt
It will give you peace; it will make you breathe
And you will feel good; just for a moment,
You will feel
Give it to me; I'll make it beautiful tonight
I'll make it perfect
I'll make it mine.
—A poem from K's old diary—1988

11:00 a.m. On A Very Hot Day

"How to Fight Loneliness" by Wilco

IT WAS A BIKINI day, but K could not wear shorts or a summer dress because of a bad fall she took while jogging around the block earlier that morning. Her knees still hurt and bled. It would be too hideous.

She would have worn a dress that day, to feel pretty, to feel more "LA," with a hint of Courtney Love, the feminine touch of a see-through, swirling skirt and unlaced Doc Martens. She went for the red and dark blue grungy, striped T-shirt instead, which made her feel somehow comfortable, yet cool. She wore it with gray skinny jeans, and black, knee-high boots she had bought in London a couple of months earlier.

K was dying from the sudden, out-of-season heat wave. She would start breathing properly only around 6:00 p.m., while waiting for the bus at the corner of Wilshire and Robertson Boulevard. Her tired feet needed some rest, and she sat on an iron bench next to a funny and long-bearded man, proudly smoking a nasty, grape-flavored cigar.

She would remember that hot day as the last one surrounded by what she liked to call the bus discomfort. She was done with it. The apartment K had just moved into with Carrie was actually a pretty good deal as a starting point, but she needed a car. The long-bearded man looked at her scarred arms.

"Is that why you did it?" The doctor at the private clinic where she was about to be hospitalized for what they called a "bulimic and self-harming tendency," asked K. He pointed at the thick scar on her right wrist.

"I don't know what you are talking about," K replied, not really sure he would believe her. She was eager to leave this hospital in the heart of Tuscany, surrounded by beautiful pine trees.

"I'm here because I don't eat. That's just another scar. I don't do that anymore," she lied. Her hands were shaking and digging small holes into much older scars on both her arms. She was scared about the consequences of the blade; it was the only thing she was really ashamed of. Food and drugs had not really caused such a sense of shame, but the wounds on her arms and on her legs truly made her look mental in her own eyes. She felt like a patient ready to be hospitalized.

"Young lady, I am a doctor," he said more like a father than a psychiatrist. The attitude bothered K, who felt threatened by the possibility of a cure. "I can see the difference. We will discuss this issue later on."

"There's nothing to be discussed," K finally spoke up. "I am not going to stay here. I am over eighteen and I can make my own decisions."

"You asked your parents to take you here," the doctor reminded her. "And it's because you know you need help. That's what we are here for, to help people like you."

"Well," K hesitated. "I've changed my mind. I think I can recover by myself. It's been a rough year, but high school is over. I just need some time."

She couldn't admit it, not even to herself. But that cut represented the beginning of K's steepest fall. The deep, thick, white vertical scar—her biggest failure. It wasn't even hard to lie at the hospital emergency room, where she had had to run, unable to stop the bleeding when the wound had gotten infected.

"It's thicker because I covered it with a leather bracelet," she explained. The doctor knew what had happened. "It got infected. They had to reopen it. They had to clean it up and put stitches on it. Not such a big deal, as you can see."

Bill was the only other person who knew the truth. One day the pain inside had just become too much to handle. And her usually innocent wounds were not enough anymore. She did try. She was very committed, too. She knew just where to cut, where to plunge the blade. What had stopped K's hand from killing her was not the thought of the pain she would cause to those who—despite what she believed—loved her. What had stopped K was an inability to make the final decision. Too cowardly to die, she had failed. That's why she kept punishing herself slowly. She wanted to suffer a greater pain, while being alive against her will. It was a reminder: More discipline could have put an early end to the self-loathing.

* * *

BILL TOLD ME TO *stick around and I trusted him. Because I was a writer? A rare natural? What the hell was I thinking that day?* The voice started torturing her. *Am I really listening to his words?*

She was supposed to work as a journalist for only six months, a year maybe, to build her résumé and get a visa. The press agency she had committed herself to was not a serious job. She never saw a future there.

Apparently, deep inside, there was still a small part of her heart hoping and dreaming of something big.

Unfortunately, I never met her. Bill was by her side during one of the most important years of her life. That is how I'm able to speak her words and take you on this journey. I am observing reality through her eyes, in between heaven and hell.

"Wild Horses" by The Rolling Stones

AFTER WORKING ALL MORNING on a new article for the promotion of a rock festival about to take place on the Sunset Strip, she turned the computer off and headed to Venice Beach for a run, where sunglasses and her Walkman were the only accessories required. K had just rented a new car, her first automatic, and after initially mistaking the brakes for the clutch on a very busy street, she wanted to feel the adrenaline of a freeway still affected by the earthquake damage, and the sweet-and-sour breeze of the ocean on her skin. She experienced a sense of freedom and accomplishment driving through the Los Angeles traffic.

Pretty confident about her new driving skills, she bottled some fresh water with lemon and left in her rented black Toyota. There was no traffic at two in the afternoon on the I-10 west. So she was able to enjoy the ride, Metallica playing loud, windows down.

Yes! I did the right thing, she thought, watching Los Angeles becoming smaller and smaller behind her in the rearview mirror, getting closer and closer to the ocean.

The Zeppelin was in the air, she started the Venice story. *I smelled Woodstock. But I didn't see the Venice I thought I would, the sunny one I remember from the movies, where palm trees are standing proud in the sky like a top model on the catwalk for Dior.*

She didn't worry about how she looked, all sweaty with messy hair in a sloppy ponytail.

There were outcasts, junkies, homeless. Venice is not what you see on a postcard when you are like me. She knew now where one of the bad parts of town was. *I could smell it, the danger and my craving came back. It had never left. If you've been there—on the other side—you are not a tourist anymore, you know what to look for. That day I tried very hard not to. I was new in town. I was scared. I liked the music and the tattoos, so I pretended it was enough. I could smell the black ink and the burning aroma of Nag Champa incense. I looked at my arms and for used needles on the beach. Where do you get a rig in Los Angeles? I kept looking around me. I knew what I needed; I knew exactly where to get it. But I smoked a cigarette instead and I went back to my stupid poetry, frustrated and sad because I was supposed to drink green tea in California, stay clean, become a new person, and do stupid Yoga.*

Venice Beach felt like an orgy, the ultimate temptation. I just wanted to crawl on the floor and forget who I was. I don't know why I didn't follow the blond guy around the corner that day. He had just what I wanted, I could read it in his eyes—words aren't necessary when you are a lost soul. I was scared, I guess. Heroin in Venice was a big step for me. I was still trying to be different, to be good. Maybe they would all love me. Or, maybe I would.

K walked back to the parking lot and cried all the way home in her new, rented Toyota.

Carrie

WHEN I MOVED FROM New York to Los Angeles in 2012, I had almost completed this manuscript about K's story, but I realized that something was missing. I tried to unveil the truth and decided to reach out to some of her closest friends in town. K's words were not enough to truly understand her. I needed the outside world to draw some of the lines and blend together K's flavors for me. I could not find K anymore. I needed to mine deeper. I wanted to find one more picture. I needed another voice that did not sound like hers or Bill's.

Some of them did not feel comfortable being a part of this book. But one did. She did not hesitate in opening up her soul and heart to me. After a very short phone call in which I barely had to say my name and that I was in Los Angeles, Carrie agreed to meet me and share her short walk of life with K.

Carrie was like a sister to K. After six months of living in Beverlywood, tired of that dirty apartment, the two of them decided to move to the Hollywood Hills. Early one morning, they started a new chapter together in the shade of the Hollywood sign, a few blocks from Griffith Park, in a beautiful two-bedroom apartment that, despite the warm, wooden furniture and rustic décor, where K hit her lowest bottom in her personal history of self-destruction.

"I was raised Amish in a small town in Ohio." Carrie started out with such a genuine smile that I instantly felt reassured. We met at Victor's Deli for lunch, just around the corner from where their apartment was, where Carrie still lives to this day—she turned K's bedroom into an art room. "I know guilt, Angie."

Carrie was in her early fifties, a blonde explosion of light, all dolled up with feathers and a variety of shades of tangerine, gold, and red. To me, she looked way younger—K had had the same impression when they had met for the first time.

"But I know her family, how was that possible?" I pointed out.

"You know what the higher meaning is, Angie?"

"Don't we all have one?"

"Yes, but the last judgment can be a threat if you don't free the soul from the written words. I have something for you."

She reached for my hand across the table to hand me a yellow piece of paper. She opened my hand and passed along what was written on it.

"K left it in her bedroom when she moved out," Carrie explained, "and after reading it, I thought I should keep it, just in case. I never got the chance to give it back to her."

"For all these years?" I asked, polite yet quite surprised. I put aside my almost-untouched plate of matzah ball soup and opened the letter, hoping for a new piece of the puzzle that was becoming harder and harder to put together or put away.

"I thought about giving it to Bill, at first. But then I completely forgot I had it, until you called me. I never thought I would actually meet you. I was very surprised when you contacted me. But you made me very happy. You look beautiful. This is some of her poetry; she didn't speak our language when it came to these matters or to life in general, as far as I know."

"I've been reading her diary, Carrie. I guess writing was just her way to protect herself. Bitter became sweeter." My smile was shy, but sincere.

"Read this," she encouraged me, "and you will understand what I am talking about."

She got up and put on her red cardigan, then the scarf, bright orange, careful not to clutch in her platinum blonde hair.

"I'm going outside for a quick smoke. I'll be right back."

As soon as I was left alone, the small table by the window became my lectern, with a view of the parking lot and a soft light shining on K's memories. The restaurant was almost empty, lunchtime had been over for a while, and I plunged into her confessions again.

Although I had felt comfortable with Carrie from the very beginning, I appreciated her allowing me some privacy with her after-meal nicotine craving. It gave me the time to gather my thoughts and put myself back together for another piece of K's history—an undated letter K wrote sometime in 1994. The letter had never been sent.

It's a birthmark on my skin.

It doesn't really matter if the Scriptures aren't your absolute truth. Your mystical aftertaste of Bible and ancient prayers still echoes loudly when I try to sleep and dusk has turned to dark.

It's either right or wrong and you made sure I would remember forever.

You are like me, there's no gray.

I thought imprinting was for birds. But it soaks in deep.

I'm still a sinner in your presence.

Show me heaven or let me know, because I know hell and it won't let me go.

Where are you?

I'm walking through the pages of a myth that I don't need And I am running past the soil of what it used to be.

I have no truth but yours to believe in.

And that's why I keep shooting, and duly giving in.

Carrie came back from her cigarette break. She took care of the check and we walked outside together. I spent a couple of hours with her and I could understand why their friendship became so important to K. Carrie knew what to do. She treasured the gift of silence when needed—a little witch and a little Zen in a sparkly mix of enthusiasm, innocence, and unconditional love.

We said goodbye like we were not sure whether a second time would come our way or not.

"You should keep it; it belongs to you." She said, when I tried to give her the poem back. "I'm sure you need it more than I do."

Maybe she saw how I desperately held onto it. She caressed my hair, as a mother would do, and she watched me walk to my car with K's words in my hands.

The more I look at them, stupid couples who think they are in love, walking by the beach, in their 300 dollar sweatshirts, holding hands, fake smiles, she wrote, *the more I know why I keep doing this to myself. I will never settle for that lie! I can't do that.*

I miss him. He was different from the other men I had been with. I'm drinking again and I went back to Venice, of course. The blond guy was still there, and I was a little less scared.

Why would you buy a 300 dollar sweatshirt to run on the beach? They don't really have any respect for money, and for how hard it is to earn it.

I chose not to feel, and I know why I did it.
I don't belong. It doesn't matter where I end up walking.
I'm never there and my skin does not fit in.
My head won't stop hurting.
It was not just high school. Why would I still be here?
I just chose an alternative way of bleeding,
Sometimes, you just need a day in Venice,
Sometimes, I just need to feel my bones again,
Sometimes, I just need a different kind of poison.
—From K's diary, May 26, 1994

The Muse

Edie Sedgwick (1943-1971)

She closed her eyes, forever.
Too young, too beautiful...
In the wrong place, trapped in her own skin
The wild poet was the only one who saw her heart
She ran away...
Black eyeliner, covering her big, dark brown eyes
That mask, that mask made her a star
But she was gone now...
Andy didn't cry when he found out
But his heart did
The goddess must die
Fate, fate played his cards
And the beautiful muse hadn't been strong enough...
She was gone, exactly how it was supposed to be

Deep, in the most tearing and suffocating pain
She closed her eyes, forever
Too young, too beautiful;
In the wrong place; prisoner in her own skin.
Andy did cry, but hid behind his paints.

"(Don't Fear) The Reaper" by Blue Öyster Cult

I KNOW YOU MAY be confused by now, wondering how much time has passed since I ventured into K's life. I'm also aware that you may well start doubting the existence of a storyline to follow, but I assure you there *is*. This is the direction I have to go. I must follow her rules and her thoughts. I must portray her path as she roamed it: randomly, passionately,with bitter brutality. It is the only direction we can take to get there, where it all will end, where everything will soon unfold. We'll find out together.

K's diaries were so vividly painted that I couldn't add much to her detailed feelings and descriptions. That is why, at times, I feel like K wrote this book herself. I am just someone she touched with her soul. I am merely giving back what was hers in the first place, what she lost many years ago: freedom.

Her inconstancy in life also spread to her journal. The diary went straight to a random Saturday morning when she was still living in Beverlywood—a predominantly Jewish neighborhood. Not being Jewish or a fan of rules in general, she ignored the fact that it was shabbat, woke up at 6:00 a.m. for a run and, like every seventh day of the Hebrew week, slalomed in between religious families walking the streets to the synagogue. She had always had a thing for the Jewish culture and tradition, she had always found their story and background interesting, sad, and melancholic. Perhaps that's why she connected so deeply with Bill.

Not that he is really religious, K wrote, introducing some early details about him on her diary. *He is more of a spiritual guy, I guess. But he is charming and depressed. His skin is damaged, sexy.*

Where Bedford Street turned into the bigger and more chaotic Pico Boulevard, her morning run transformed into an interesting and historical ride made of Torah, kippah, and payot, as commanded in Leviticus 19:27.

Running was another addiction that gave her power.

You know that kind of powerful feeling you get when you're high on cocaine? For the first ten minutes of glory? Or the first hours of warm euphoria when shooting heroin? Real power, like Scotch neat. It's a confident mask when you don't have your drugs to temporarily delete unwanted memories of being you. Just like the bullshit you want to believe in to stay alive, or to get your check-out from reality. I don't want to be aware.

When she had decided she would try to quit drugs, months before, she had gone back to her primary addiction, to her primary source of control: the adrenaline of emptiness inside her body.

If she had to go out and put clothes on her hated body, she had to run first, to feel right, to fit in her place in the world. To somehow get another fix that would help her handle breathing.

It was a nightmare, nothing but a bad dream she couldn't wake up from. Physically she did not feel good. What she had been noticing lately was the inability to analyze and properly perceive every single inch of the uncomfortable weight she had to carry and drag with her. She thought she had changed, over those few months in Los Angeles.

After a quick shower, K got dressed and smoked a cigarette.

On a regular day, she would have stayed hidden in her own shelter of pain until the day after, when the punishment would be over. But this time, she couldn't even think about it. Her life in California was supposed to be different, and she was really putting all her efforts in to making the change happen.

Her friend picked her up at 11:00 a.m. and they drove straight to Santa Monica. She was not used to having any kind of food before 5:00 p.m., especially when out with people. But sushi was allowed, and K managed to get through the discomfort of putting rice into her mouth in front of a whole restaurant.

"I don't want lunch." She suddenly recalled screaming at her mother. "Stop asking!"

"Why don't you eat during the day?" K's nutritionist asked when trying to establish a new diet plan for a hopeless patient. K was twenty.

"Do I really have to waste time and explain? What do you know? You are thin."

"I work with people like you, K, and I just want to help you."

"People like me? What do you think I am? Some spoiled white girl that wants to be a top model? I can't eat, okay? I need the water to flow freely. I feel dirty when I eat. I just can't. You don't know what happens if I do."

"What do you see in the mirror after you have a meal? Nothing changes after a meal, K. You need about nine thousand calories to gain something like two pounds."

"Well, for me it does. You don't know what I see and how much it hurts," she said, while tears started streaming down her face to the point where she could barely speak. "Just stop, please. You will never understand."

"K, listen to me," the sweetest voice said. The nutritionist handed her a Kleenex. "You have to trust me."

"Do you want me to go to school and be able to walk around during the day? Well, stop asking me to eat. After five p.m., I don't have to be around people anymore, and I then eat."

"Let's hear, what do you eat after five?"

"Something. But that's none of your business. I was sent here because I apparently don't eat, and I just proved you wrong. I'm out of here!"

Imagine your wounded hand down your bleeding throat. That shadow of shame and disgust that makes you want to die, right there, curled up on the humid and dirty floor of a public bathroom. K wrote upon returning home from her Santa Monica outing, not quite sure she was relieved for not relapsing and getting rid of the sushi. *I was that girl in tears with the black eyeliner melting on my face; I tasted bile and acetone. That taste that you don't simply rinse off with a Wintergreen Altoid. It was a mix of vinegar and milk gone bad.*

She remembered everything. K's mind still dwelled in those days of self-destruction and extreme cleansing. Every house she had lived in but one, so far, had been marked with that memory—bulimia. The only reason why one house had remained off the list was because the man that lived in it managed to set K up with a fix of a different nature: alcohol, drugs, and a sexual addiction to a love that was never there.

When K did not have money, she would rummage through the trash; in between dirt and ash, she would find a piece of stale bread, apple peels, and some boiled pasta—the remains of a previous binge.

Sometimes not even the trash bin was by my side, she cried on paper, desperate to be heard, *and the only food I had was flour, cane sugar, and chlorine-smelling tap water. A whole pack of flour, and I ate it all, until my stomach hurt so bad I almost couldn't stand up straight anymore. I had to crawl to the bathroom to find the only possible relief. It's a matter of purification and punishment for not being strong enough. That's how I'd survive the hate towards myself. I would drink all the hot and salty water I could hold in my body, only to throw it up, for hours sometimes, until the blood was the only color I could see coming out of my wounded mouth.*

Once those hours were over, it was time for judgment to take the lead.

I would look, disgusted and disappointed, at myself in the mirror until my face did not even make sense anymore. Sarah was right.

One of her favorite parts was about to begin. Cutting her arms deeper and deeper with her favorite, threaded, black knife, until she could see that yellow part of flesh that told her she was getting closer to the end. She would stop there, because cowardice was somehow stronger than death and willpower. The only prayer she could speak out loud those nights was for her heartbeat to stop, once and for all.

"My sins are being washed away." She cried in her mind, scratching her arm with her red fingernails. That's what she kept saying to Dr. Carmen.

"What sins, K?"

"It washes them away, so I can sleep."

"You don't have sins to be forgiven, Sweetheart. You are just punishing yourself, and for no reason," the doctor tried to explain, with no real hope for K to finally embrace that truth.

"You don't understand!" K screamed.

"When you are being shown things are wrong with you, for years and years, you end up proving them right." She justified with such a tone that she sounded like a psychology textbook; anybody could see the ghost she had become.

"I must empty myself when I'm about to blow up; the relief is chemical. Do you even know what I'm talking about? That I need to purify my blood? That I need to feel transparent? I should be locked up somewhere, because I don't even make sense to myself anymore. The other day I poured ammonia on trashed food; I thought it would prevent me from doing it, but it didn't work. I ate it anyway, and then threw up. Once it starts, this thing in my brain, I can't stop it. What am I without it?"

Gemma

"She stole it from me," she revealed for the very first time—her mother's biggest mistake.

"Wasn't being blonde, thin, and beautiful enough? I could smell it from my bedroom after dinner, when she pretended her metabolism was fast and she was the lucky one in the family, the one who did not gain weight. Did she really think I was stupid and didn't understand what was going on? One day she had five slices of cake and four glasses of wine! You don't binge on wine, by the way. I studied the rules. I don't know…I feel like she watched me disappear, when I was starving, and then she stabbed me in the back. There was a time when she was concerned about me. I miss that.

"When my mother discovered I was bulimic, she thought her daughter was really sick, lost forever. My parents did not even know about eating disorders when everything started. And, sometimes I think my mother became jealous of all the attention I was getting.

"You talked about playing the victim: Where do you think I learned? I know that you don't have a daughter, but would you steal the pain from one of your sons to feel more important?"

"Why don't you talk to her, K? Why don't you bring your mother here, to therapy? It could help you both. Resentment will only make it worse. You will end up hating yourself more than you hate her."

"I'm not ready to face her. And she still does it every night after dinner, when we are watching the news in religious silence. You don't dare talk during the news in our house, or my father will start a fight.

"So, as we sit and ignore each other's truth, she eats more, and more, and she can't stop. Just like me. Althoug, I do it alone, in the middle of the night, when no one can see me. I would rather throw up in a plastic bag than be seen.

"She performs so well that they all believe her lies, her innocent silence.

"I never thought I was capable of hating. But I have come very close to the feeling. And to fight the hate, I learned indifference. I do love her still, she is my mother, after all, she's never let me down; but I can't forgive her for what she did to me."

Once started, she couldn't stop herself. She continued to talk to the doctor. But it didn't help the healing.

"And my brother seems to be blind, too. They all live in denial, because she does it before their eyes and in my family you can deal with conscience, philosophy, and politics. But shame? Shame must be buried."

If shame was to be buried deep in the frosted soil of the Northern Alps, or hidden behind a family portrait, her mother's secret had to be, as well. She would never give Gemma the satisfaction of offering help, a talk, or recovery. K ignored her mother's health, the issues were too many to fix. In order to survive, get by, understanding how close she was to forever losing Gemma was not in the cards.

"She is almost fifty," K said, expert on all the medical causes of death for bulimia nervosa—she could die. "You don't need the science. Your heart stops beating one day, with your fingers still covered in acid and spit, and a scar on your hand that never heals. She could die and now I know what my sin is: I don't care. With my luck she will die in style, while I have to beg for death in vain, on my knees.

"She will die and they will cry. And I'll still be here, shadow of her fucking wound, dragging her former beauty for the years to come.

"If recovery was ever an option for me, I'm done. Not leaving it to her. Sorry."

Santa Monica, 1994

BACK IN THE SUSHI restaurant restrooms, in Santa Monica, she took a deep breath. She knew it. It was Hollywood, the bulimia capital of perfection and hidden ruin. She thought about how she had always shared drugs but purging and hurting herself were acts to be performed alone, in the darkness of her home. *You try not to do it in an elegant restaurant in Santa Monica, and if you have to, because it happens, when you are forced by the circumstances of life, you learn to be silent. There are tricks for it. I really don't want to hear you, triggering me, vomiting your lunch.*

Those were the most terrifying moments she had experienced in a long time. K shivered, like she had been offered a dose for free. She tried to resist with all her strength, while already tasting it in her mouth, feeling the relief with her brain.

A part of her wanted to get out of there, forget about it, but she could not even move. She was paralyzed, standing on a fragile, very dangerous line.

Do it, K! The voice inside her head screamed. *Do it! Do it, and you'll feel perfect! Remember clean. Remember white. Do it! Prove you're worth your label. Do it, K.*

Five minutes that seemed like five hours passed. It felt like torture. She could taste the ecstasy and feel the guilt. K tasted it, the blood in her mouth, the sweet-and-sour fluid of a pain she wasn't ready to bid farewell to.

"Post Blue" by Placebo

PURGING AND BLEEDING WERE not her only ways of hurting herself. Drugs were part of it, too. K was very democratic when it came to suffering. She did not care about the ingredients. The nature of her fix had never been precisely an issue.

She almost never used to get high to have fun, except on rare occasions, at the very beginning, a teenager trying to fit in, lying about who she really was or, more likely, desperate to escape the life she had been given, for no reason. Drugs are fun when you are a freshman addict, before you know you are one.

The first time I had sex after blowing cocaine with my boyfriend? How can I forget that power? I finally felt free and realized I could be much more than who I really was. I am

not going to lie, I hated myself. I felt ugly and inappropriate.
I didn't know how to be with a man. My first and last had
been Alex; I didn't know what love was. And drunk or high,
I felt okay, almost perfect, every hurt disappeared. I knew
how to move my body on theirs. I could be what they wanted
me to be. I felt like I could live forever.

With many of them I never came. I rarely had an
orgasm. But I didn't care about my own pleasure as long
as I could hold those men in-between my legs, in my life.
That was my power. I became so good at it that I probably
should have chosen sex as a career, instead of opening an
interior design boutique, or trying to become an interpreter.
I found myself deeply in debt, but very skilled in the art of
multiple orgasm and pleasure giving, as long as I was loaded
or wasted. I was their elegant escort in a restaurant, their
wife in the kitchen, and their whore in bed. I could rarely
be a friend. As long as I said yes to anything they wanted,
everything was fine. And for a long time I thought I was, too.

K truly believed she was smart enough to have power
and control over it. But she did not know that she was
just a slave, about to graduate in the art of telling lies and
obliterating feelings. Parties and loud music were fun
until nine o'clock in the morning with no sleep, rivers
of tequila coursing through her. She danced restless and
drunk in the streets of Turin, sweating the nights away in
her favorite spots. By the river, where music was loud and
sex was free, she became popular, a sexy queen with no
limits and no control. In K's mind, those nights of dark
circles under her eyes and high heels on her feet were the

best revenge against those that had always thought of her as the fat and ugly kid from across the railroad tracks. She thought she was living a reality show made of black eyeliner and illusory victory. At first, she could handle drugs and stay clean during the day, but everything changed the first morning she got high to wake up and be presentable at work. Cocaine had become a toxic substitute for coffee and make up, a white line and a phone card on her bedside table.

Since that very first daylight high, everything started to change. She started using to control food and to feel something when she was lost and empty. Other drugs started helping her to flush away her feelings when she was overwhelmed by emotions, when the awareness of the day would hurt her too much. They would warm the body and relax the brain, slowing down the heartbeat. Others would just help her sleep the pain away and eventually forget by washing away entire days and entire nights she would never remember again. K started to rely on every fix she could find in order to escape the boundaries of her own mind, but it was never enough.

Because that is what lies are for. To betray, to deceive the small and mediocre world we inhabit into believing that we are somebody else, someone better, or something more.

Nights became entire days and fun turned into fear, hallucinations, fever, fornication, and paranoia.

I always had a plate full of cocaine in my closet, K wrote, *and no matter how full that plate was I saw it empty. I was blowing from it and I was worrying it would become empty again. That's how I would spend my days. Staring*

paranoid at a plate of cocaine. *The plate was always full, but
to me the plate looked always empty. Nothing else mattered
except keeping that plate full. Twenty-four hours a day. It's
the most exhausting thought I've ever experienced in my
whole life: how to keep a plate full when you constantly need
to empty it.*

It was a sunshiny summer afternoon in Los Angeles, K
continued, on the same page. *I was alone in my apartment
and, like every morning, cocaine was the only thing to get me
out of bed at 7:00 a.m. to write the news. It didn't matter if I
was hallucinating by that time. I thought LAPD helicopters
were looking for me because my visa was about to expire. I
would hide in the closet for hours with my plate of cocaine.
I didn't care. I desperately needed it to get dressed and start
writing. Every night I would prepare my plate with four or
five thick and beautifully designed white lines and a piece
of straw; I needed it to function, to put on a T-shirt and be
the person that people wanted me to be. I just had to stretch
my arm and reach for the plate waiting for me, a couple of
inches from my bed. Only then I could walk into the world.*

Every ten minutes, I needed more; there were days
when Carrie worked at the desk next to mine in our
living room and I could barely hide it. That's when I
moved the typewriter to my bedroom, to have my plate
of cocaine on the other work table, so I didn't even have
to walk from one room to another to get it, and she
would not have to notice my walking back and forth,
my nose bleeding and my breathing getting worse by
the minute. But that day something seemed different,

she continued; her writing changing all of a sudden, switching from a black ink pen to soft pencil.

Nothing went wrong for a while. My using schedule at that time was still very strict; I was a control freak, after all. My rule during that time was to have the last line no later than 8:00 p.m., because I needed to be able to switch drugs, to collapse and sleep at night, and to be able to work the morning after, like a regular person. I wasn't partying. Cocaine had become a very solitary hell.

That scary day was nothing different from her daily routine, until the moment K's nose stopped delivering air. And shooting it into her arm was the only option to get through the next hour. That's how much she needed it.

I didn't know what to do. I panicked. My heart raced, and stupid as I was, my fear was not related to the fact that I could die. I couldn't snort anymore, my only priority and reason for living. It wasn't supposed to happen!

I decided to take a break from it. I had some codeine and I took it with Xanax; I loved that mix. I just needed to relax and everything would be fine.

That's what I thought, while lying down on the floor, giving myself a Reiki treatment. I put my hands on the heart chakra. My mother says that everything can be fixed with Reiki. I didn't have anything to lose. What an image: a cokehead doing Reiki to do more blow.

The fever got higher. I remember seeing a black cat biting my arm, and he wouldn't go away. I started screaming!

Carrie knocked on my door and the cat finally disappeared. I knew I was crazy, but never to this extent! I wasn't a fucking junkie, right?

I guess an hour or so went by and I wanted more cocaine. I tried, but my nose started bleeding again and nothing would go up.

I had a photograph of my grandmother next to where I was desperately trying to snort my line. I don't even know why I had moved the plate to the bookshelf, where she was.

Shame was the only feeling I could perceive and yet I did not cry. I was stronger that that. My grandmother had died. She had left me without an instruction manual on how to live this life I hated. I tried again, moving the plate away from her. But my nose did not work. The membrane was so swollen that I couldn't even breathe, there was no way I could snort it. I smoked it at first, but it wasn't enough. I couldn't feel it anymore. So I prepared my arm. I felt safe again. I was very careful, and once I had found the vein I knew everything would be fine. When everything was over, my article written and delivered, I was exhausted. The high slowly turned into a deep coma, with high fever again.

I looked at my grandmother and felt ashamed, so guilty for how much I had disappointed her. I just couldn't bear her eyes anymore. It was probably seven thirty in the evening when I took more Xanax and my bottle of vodka.

I closed my eyes and waited to collapse.

I was hallucinating. I needed to sleep. I needed to forget the evidence of even existing. The helicopters were still there, but the voices disappeared, and I started to lose perception of my body.

I had gone too far, one more time. Yet, more would come.

For a minute she thought about getting clean, but the Xanax kicked in and she finally blacked out, completely forgetting about her good intentions. She had not showered in days and her skin was gray. Even the best concealer couldn't cover the red spots on her forehead and chin.

The weeks that followed the lunch danger were silent, with no writing. I looked for her words, but the only trace of her I was left with was a tattoo and a burned piece of yellow paper from her purple leather appointment calendar.

They say despair and solitude help the creative process, yet the despair part is often a myth that can lead you to death. K's pain was so excruciating at times that she did not even know if she could go on. When your head is so loud, words do not come. You cannot move and pray for a sign. You cannot breath, so you pray for air, motionless. And, if the sign comes, you can't see it. She didn't.

Full Moon

It was June, and K was overwhelmed by the many new assignments at the press agency.

On a full moon night, she decided to take a break from writing and from preparing boring interviews with actors of TV shows she couldn't care less about. She closed the dictionary by her side and spotted a flyer printed on blue paper: "Swing By…" it read in gold. "Moonlight Shadow on The Pacific. 5:30-Midnight. FREE."

A shirt hung from one of the armrests. K picked it up and glimpsed at her figure in the mirror. She detested her body and there wasn't anything that could have helped her to see it as anything but disgusting.

Back in the sixties, her grandmother was hospitalized and given electroshock therapy, for trying to kill her demons, the same ones K was trying to escape. She knew everything about it from Silvia's diaries. K had read them all after Silvia had passed away. The story of a woman who had lived through World War I and World War II, who loved mathematics, yet had been forced to work in a sewing machine factory because that's what women did.

Silvia and K had a lot in common. She was the most sensitive and delicate woman K had ever known. The two of them always had a special connection, because of their mental symptoms and because Silvia gave her the maternal figure she took for granted in her own mother. K understood why, years later, when her relationship with Gemma was on life-support. She missed both of them in that moment, but only the relationship with her mother could still be saved. Silvia was gone forever. And the guilt of the unspoken words, of the pain she had caused her with her drunken behavior, was killing K.

That night there was a full moon and part of an artistic community that K had met a few weeks earlier in Los Angeles was gathering in Malibu, by the ocean, for a New Age ritual after one of their bands played live.

They were not K's cup of tea, but she had connected with a couple of them for work reasons and a guy named Tim had invited her to see the show, which she decided to write about. Malibu was not their normal scene, they usually gathered in the Franklin Village, at the bottom of the Hollywood Hills. The neighborhood sat in the shadow of the Hollywood sign, where the controversial, gothic-style Church of Scientology stands proud and powerful; the Celebrity Centre on Franklin Avenue surrounded by sharp contrasts made of small New York-style cafés, hippie clothing boutiques, art galleries, theaters, and an old charming bookstore, where the 1978 original manuscript of Hubert Selby's *Requiem for a Dream* is, today, up to 150 dollars.

K never thought she could go to an event like this by herself: a new city, no guide or companion, she barely knew these people. Most of them she had met by chance, through common friends or because she had listened to their music in one of the Beachwood bars, where most of them lived at the time. *There will be wine,* she thought. *And the ocean.*

She took three Xanax and walked in. The place was stunning, and despite the traffic, she had made it in time to relish a breathtaking sunset on the Pacific. The event took place on the Japanese-inspired terrace, right on the ocean. The restaurant, known to be the ultimate surfer hangout back in the seventies, was now one of the most glamorous, romantic, and hip spots for an expensive champagne toast surrounded by waves and seafood. The wooden floor and the white curtains made it look it like a beach house, warmed only by scented, cream-colored candles, and furnished with elegant and simple chaise lounges and bamboo tables. With a glass of pinot gris in one hand and a Gauloises cigarette in the other, she allowed herself to get lost.

If you have never felt the power of the ocean, you should be aware of what it really is. For it is much more than seawater. It's majesty. The ocean is powerful, to such an extent that it almost fights the sky to overtake the whole space in between. It cannot get enough. When you experience the sun dying into its waters, you perceive its power over fire. That's how she described it on a piece of toilet paper that was attached to the page of diary from that same night. K could not bear the presence of people for too long. Somehow she had to escape and hide to gather her thoughts. The small clutch she had decided to wear that night could not fit a notebook, and she found toilet paper in the restrooms to write on. *It is the ocean's water that rules the shades of color. It is the water that decides how to reflect and paint each drop of sun's blood melting into it. It is the water that cherishes the elegance and the magic of the silvery queen, the moon. The ocean has all the power, and I can inhale it. Like getting high on its essence.*

That night K tried to let the gentle breeze heal and caress both her body and her soul for a little while. She spent most of the evening by herself, sitting on a bench drinking wine and just listening to the waves until midnight came, and it was time to drive back home.

On her way back to Los Angeles, the full moon reflected its shimmery light on the ocean. K drove as slowly as she could to enjoy the miracle and the feeling of pride for what she had just done, showing up and walking the streets alone. K had won the battle against the cruel part of her brain, even if just for a couple of hours.

Bill

J ust two days from the self-confidence of the ocean night, on the Sunday morning that followed, K's only thought was killing herself. She wanted to cut up the body she hated so much; she could not bear waking up sad anymore.

She was so consumed by remorse and the important decisions she kept having to make that she felt like she was completely losing control. She took two Xanax, which did not work. She was trying not to go back to heavy drugs again. So she took one more, but something was wrong, she couldn't feel it. Her body didn't react to it.

The voice inside my head gets louder and louder and I can't help but listening to it, K's pen tried to explain again, *the voice is the only presence I have by my side. It's the only one that will never leave me. It's the only one I can always go back to, anytime, with no explanation or excuse.*

On her body, K had always reversed all her fears, all her doubts, disappointments and mistakes, so much so that it had become a cemetery of feelings. She couldn't take it anymore. Not that morning. The more she stared at the image reflected in the mirror, the more she hated herself for losing time and energy, concentrating so hard on something so shallow. That voice was preventing her from even going out, having a simple conversation, and just being part of the world that, whether she liked it or not, she lived in. Even her boss had started to think that she was weird. As much as she kept hiding those secrets, K wasn't as skilled as she thought at carrying out a double life.

She went out on the balcony and sat on the dusty floor, facing the courtyard. There wasn't a proper garden or a swimming pool she could look at, but a couple of skinny palm trees instead. She closed her eyes to avoid the unwanted natural surroundings and sat still for a while.

With her knees tucked to her chest, and slowly swinging her body back and forth, she let herself create the dream in detail. Death.

It was the portrait of a painful and punishing doom. Burning and destroying every inch of skin and flesh was the only relief she could find. She needed flames. She just wished for it all to be over, once for all. K wanted to die, because after a very careful evaluation of her condition, she didn't feel she deserved another chance.

"Elsa died yesterday," She told Dr. Carmen during one of her therapy sessions, with tears in her eyes.

"Who's Elsa?" Dr. Carmen asked, very kindly, almost like she knew where K's argument was headed.

"She was another patient in the eating disorder recovery program," K explained, not looking at the doctor in the eyes, but scratching her arms instead. She wasn't really sure whether what she was about to say was the right thing, "She was twenty years old—heart failure, anorexia."

K remained silent. She stared at the Doctor's degree framed on the wall before her and did not speak, until Dr. Carmen picked up the conversation again.

"Talk to me, K. I can't help you if you don't talk to me."

"I can't stop asking myself the same question, over and over again. I didn't even cry when I found out. I called her and her mother picked up the phone. Elsa hated her mother; she was a bitch. I remember when she called me in tears because her mother told her she was fat. She kept telling her she was a lost cause and she didn't care anymore if she'd live or die, eat or starve herself. Elsa was paying for her own doctors, and you know how expensive you are. You want to know what I did, after her mother told me?" K finally decided to talk, despite how ashamed she was of her actions. "I went to the grocery store and spent all the money I had in my wallet; then I ran back home and ate it all, until my stomach was so full I was barely able to walk to the bathroom, and then I finally threw up. I hadn't been throwing up for three weeks until that day. I wanted to die. I wanted to be her. I am tired."

"Why do you want to die?" Dr. Carmen said, meeting K's eyes, spilling over oppressive sadness.

"Because I don't care anymore. My friend is fucking dead and I want to be her. What kind of person am I? I asked God the reason why. Why her and not me? Why did he choose someone else, again? You know how many of my friends have overdosed? Why not me? How many fucking times have I asked that question! You have no idea. And now Elsa; because she was just like me, her heart stopped beating, while I'm still here suffering and begging. She deserved this life more than I do. Elsa was really fighting. I am not. I want to be in a hospital with an IV in my arm; she was really trying to fight it. Why do I want to be in a hospital? Why do I want to be sick and die?"

When she opened her eyes again, on the dirty balcony, with her knees tucked to her chest, exactly how she was twenty minutes before, she had to do something. The only thing she could think of to get rid of those dangerous feelings was running to the beach. That's what she did, not to burn calories but simply to resist the craving for something dangerous.

Without even realizing that the sun had finally introduced summer to Southern California for the first time that year, she covered her body with every piece of black she could find in her closet. She headed to the car wearing the darkest sunglasses she owned, hoping no one would see her.

Too many voices screamed in her head; the last thing she needed was music while driving. Silence was what she asked for, and peace, both on the outside and on the inside. Getting to Santa Monica and finding a parking spot took less time than she figured and she was soon ready to run on the beach.

Only minutes earlier, while still driving, K had meditated on her need for pain, a feeling she relied on to feel worthy of the life she had been given. Happiness frightened her more than darkness—another chain from which she didn't know how to free herself.

"Put those voices in your writing," Bill had told her. "Turn the hell into a gift. That's all we can do, the best we can do. It hurts like fuck, but it's your gift, baby. We're all in love with our own pain, scream it into the page and it will turn around. I promise. I promise baby, it will turn around."

Instead of running, she drew an image of him in her head and missed him tremendously.

"We're all in love with our own pain. Scream it into the page and it will turn around. I promise baby, it will turn around."

As soon as she started to think about their story, K wished she had a pen and a piece of paper. She wanted and needed to run, but the stream of words and memories became so impetuous that she went back to the car and wrote what happened on several paper napkins she found in the dashboard, next to coffee and lipstick stains.

* * *

"Chelsea Hotel No. 2" by Leonard Cohen

IT WAS THE BEGINNING of March, 1994, the third, to be precise, during that very first press conference K covered for the Italian magazine, while staying at the hotel in Koreatown with no car and just a map to wander around town. Bill was the star, the genius writer, the man she was supposed to interview, who ended up digging into K's life instead, completely changing the course of events in the adventure that she had just embarked on.

The first moment she saw him, she felt it. Bill Werber was his name. He was much older than her, but so handsome that she almost couldn't breathe when they were introduced by his publicist. He was born in 1938 to Jewish parents that emigrated from Russia in the late twenties.

After leaving the States for a writing pilgrimage through Europe, Bill lived in New York for a while, and then moved to Los Angeles in the early sixties to pursue his writing career, and unsuccessfully take a break from the dangerous road he was roaming back East, in those years when drugs were cheap and jazz a dead end road. It was the Beat Generation and then the Vietnam Era and Bill was a burning fire of repressed anger and pain.

"I have my own spirituality," he used to say with an addictive, tormented smile on his face, "but I'm just an old Jew inside. There's nothing I can do; happiness is not part of my biological heritage, I guess."

"I went to Europe when I was twenty," he told me one day when I asked him about an old photo I had found in K's diary, "it was nineteen fifty-eight when I went to Greece. I stayed there a while and studied the classics; then I traveled to Italy and France by train. But Salamis Island was beautiful, Euripides was born there, I guess was hoping to get some inspiration by osmosis. I went from silence to chaos to solve the same dilemma," he continued, "but neither of them worked. So, I ended up coming back to America, enriched with culture but even more chaotic inside, with the same burden and a very expensive need for crack, cocaine, and eventually heroin."

Bill came back from the United Kingdom and moved to California in 1963, never to return to his hometown, except once, briefly, in 1965 for his mother's funeral. His father had committed suicide when he was fifteen and his older sister had already left the country and moved to India to find her true self with the Hare Krishna, then open an orphanage with her second husband after three years of chanting, a rigorous vegetarian diet, and extreme yoga practices.

Bill's beauty is unconventional, dark, and complicated. He is damaged in the most dangerous and intriguing sense. For the press conference, he chose a casual attire of gray stonewashed jeans and a black loose-fitting shirt that perfectly caressed his thin-yet-vigorous body. He has signs on his pale skin: signs of life, signs of self-loathing. And his eyes are so deep that I could hardly concentrate on the job I was paid to do.

He did not talk a lot, mainly listening and managing to balance his public figure with his mysterious and solitary nature.

His voice was deep, irreverent, sexual, and warm. You know when you get close to having an orgasm? Her wobbling hand recalled, *that's the effect he had on my brain and on my body. His rough and calm voice was a slow and rhythmic acoustic orgasm. He knew it, and he played with it, in front of my adoring eyes.*

While everyone in the room was having a lunch catered by some fancy gourmet Beverly Hills restaurant, he just asked for some water and elegantly grabbed an apple from the fruit basket. He did not smile. Bill did not look at ease, and she could feel his discomfort. The Beverly Hills luxury was not his scene, and neither were the Hollywood glow, the arrogance of a power-drunk producer, or the entitlement of those rich people pretending to be more than they really were. That world was not his thing. He was simply a writer, and seemed to be annoyed by any unnecessary accessory to his own art.

Bill was the screenwriter of a new thriller scheduled to be released in theaters a couple of days later. The plot was tedious and unoriginal, so they called him; he knew how to transform stupid bullshit into an interesting and controversial piece of art. That's why his followers loved him so much, because he did not fear the critics' judgment. Writing seemed to be easier than life, and he just needed to do it, not for fame, but to handle a sober life. It was sometimes like looking in a mirror for K because Bill's past was rough and bitter. He had been a heroin addict for more than twenty years, and when he got sober, more dead than alive, he ended up with an incurable form of Hepatitis C, which was making his existence more miserable every day. No matter how successful he had become in Hollywood through the years, like any addict, he would always be one. And K was about to know it well.

Bill had lost everything to heroin, cocaine, and crack. He had risked his life and that of his kid, until he finally decided to get sober and turn his life around, to become the man he was the day he met K. Just what she needed, nothing different from what she was used to dealing with, and apparently nothing different from what she was really looking for: danger, some form of romantic torment.

He looked lost in the hotel room, and his discomfort helped make K fit into the scene (she was the one who was supposed to feel lost, having just arrived, young, under the gun, and in an environment that was not naturally hers). Somehow, he naturally managed to make her feel up to the task. Bill looked at her arms, covered with tattoos and deep scars, almost like he was attracted to them. He noticed her in some way, and next to each other in that hotel room, an unexpected sexual chemistry took over, a dangerous tension filled the air. K couldn't remember the last time she had felt such a sentiment for a man.

She knew perfectly well he was old for her. He could be her father. But she did not even think about it in that moment.

Besides his enigmatic allure, he seemed to have a smart, dry sense of humor. In fact, in a very subtle way he made fun of the project itself. The interview was supposed to be set in order to let Bill express his own idea of the movie, to explain how he had managed to turn the plot into something breathtaking, scandalous, and well-built, but in almost two hours, he had only spoken a couple of times. For the remaining part of the afternoon, his eyes were just concentrated on the small black diary he was writing in and, of course, on K.

She loved the way he reported everything in his little black notebook. Apparently, he was writing every single detail catching his attention and K wondered, just for one second, if he was also writing about her on those small and aged pages of his. She secretly hoped so, but she was losing focus, and she was there to work.

When the press conference was over, Bill approached K as she was grabbing a last minute Earl Grey from the refreshment table. He poured himself a cup and casually broke the ice, off the record.

"Cool tattoo, what does it say?" he asked, pointing at the ink on K's left arm.

"It's Latin, Cicero," she replied. "*Nihil Inimicus Quam Sibi Ipse;* a rough translation could be…" She thought. "It means that we are our own worst enemy. Isn't it true?"

"Oh God, I wish I had done that, instead of this Celtic bullshit!" He laughed showing his, on his left shoulder. "Never get a tattoo when you're high!"

"Thank you for the tip," K said, laughing. "I'll keep that in mind. What doesn't kill you makes you wiser, uh?"

"Gentle way to put it. Very European! Which part of Italy are you from, by the way?"

"Turin, where the Shroud is, why?"

"Just curious," Bill replied. "I remember talking sex with an Italian writer a while ago, when I was in Rome.

She told me she wasn't really able to have intense orgasms when having sex in another language. Now every time I meet an Italian woman I don't think about pasta, but about the translation of an orgasm."

"Wow, nice pick-up line," she said, smiling, and blushing a little.

"Didn't want to embarrass you; it's just some old Jewish humor. Want some milk in you Earl Grey?" he said, satisfied to see her blushing.

A few words, some innocent flirting maybe, and they just stared at each other as though a miracle had just happened. They walked together to the lobby and after a couple of minutes, just before reaching for his black Corvette, he quickly wrote down a couple of books for her to read, along with his contact information.

"By the way, this is my phone number," he said, handing her a piece of paper from his notebook. "Not that I do this every time, don't get me wrong, I'm not some kind of media whore, but it was nice talking to you. Let me know if you like *White Noise*. If you like DeLillo you are going to love this one."

Not a, "Let's have coffee sometime," not a stupid excuse to see her again, just a number on such a small piece of paper that she could lose in the blink of an eye. After a stolen touch, Bill was gone.

Following the press junket, they finally met for lunch. It was two days later and K was about to run some last-minute errands in West Hollywood before checking out of the hotel and moving into the new apartment with Carrie.

She checked the map and looked for the lighter, lost somewhere in her small and messy yellow leather purse; not finding it she had to go back to her room, and there it was, a voice mail from Bill.

"Hey, I tried to call you both in your room and on your pager. If you're planning to live down here you should consider the idea of setting up a private voice mail…Anyway, I just thought I'd catch you for lunch. Call me back, if you still have my number."

She shuddered. She had not planned on seeing him that day, so soon. She was not mentally ready for it. She hurried out of the room and got on the first bus to West Hollywood. It was a long and agitated drive, because the only thing she could think about was Bill, his lips and his breath.

K got off the bus before her stop and decided to walk, to both release the tension and decide whether to call him back and meet him, or forget about it and go on with her day. She thought about what to do while walking restlessly on Melrose Avenue. She double-checked her outfit: gray skinny jeans, black velvet knee boots, and a grungy, bluish, long shirt. No make-up, a pair of old sunglasses from the eighties, and a simple touch of cherry-flavored lip balm on her lips.

Is it going to be enough for him? she thought. *But why am I even worrying about it? He's not my boyfriend and I don't have to impress him. So,* she rambled, while pretending she was interested in every store the street offered, *we might just have a coffee and talk about writing. He is a writer, after all.*

K nervously grabbed the last cigarette in the pack. She looked around to see if there was a payphone nearby and spotted one just around the block, next to a vintage furniture store and a rundown pawnshop. She walked slowly, leaving time to change her mind and consider all the options. K dug up a quarter from her change purse and looked at it as if it were some kind of oracle. She finished her cigarette and took a deep breath, looking around to make sure she was alone and that no one had followed her, almost like she was about to do something illegal. She finally dialed the number.

He didn't sound polite on the phone. Bill never seemed to be friendly, and she guessed phone calls were not his thing. But that sinister sharpness had fascinated her. She was scared, yet she couldn't wait to see him again. Bill told her to stop by Canter's on Fairfax, one of the places he loved the most.

One of the most famous delis in LA, upon walking through its doors K found herself surrounded by a dream of pastrami and chopped liver. Bill didn't know her yet, but without even trying, he had gotten the girl.

They sat at one of the front tables, dark red leather and a home-cooked deli food smell. The place wasn't crowded at two thirty in the afternoon, but she felt like all the spotlights were on them. He listened a lot; Bill was more interested in hearing about her life than in talking about his. She let herself go, showing him the darkest places she had roamed so far, letting him see her dark and scared soul.

"What did you do?" Bill asked, like it was the most natural way to start a conversation with a woman he was trying to have sex with.

"What do you mean?" she asked.

"I saw your scars, and I can see the pain, even if it's in another language."

"It's a long story," her shivering, Italian voice continued. "Tell me about you."

"Well, I have no other place to go and I'm sure you are much more interesting than an old Jew hired to fix a stupid movie."

K had no other place to go, either. That's how it all started, in an old diner with no plans or schedule, just the two of them. After talking for hours over coffee and strawberry cheesecake for her, black tea and Greek salad for him, Bill took her hand.

"You are a natural, K. You are a writer."

K did not say a word.

"You know, I don't usually do this. I don't read young writers' works. I am no one," Bill humbly said, not like some Hollywood producer who wants to fuck the girl, but like someone who was really seeing her.

"But there's something in you. That diary of yours, those poems you sent me the other night. From what I can tell, it's not just a diary. You are special."

"You don't even know me."

"You're right, I don't. But I think I know where you've been, and I see through your eyes. That's more than enough. But then again, I am no one. That's just my opinion. Let me take you back to the hotel."

"Thank you, Bill," she said, leaving the diner with him, after validating his parking ticket at the main counter on the way out.

"Of course," Bill reassured her. "And listen, I am going in the same direction, you shouldn't be taking the bus, especially when it's getting dark. I lived on public transportation in this town when I got sober the first time and didn't even have a driver's license," he continued, while they walked to his car. "When I left the treatment center I barely had the money to make a phone call. I know how that feels, trust me."

They walked to the Canter's parking lot around the corner. He opened the door of his Corvette for her, and they drove down Fairfax Avenue with some low-volume radio that helped build up the tension to the perfect height for that day. After a quick stop at the Beverly Wilshire to pick up a couple of books from a friend of his, they headed towards Koreatown. It was while already driving east on Wilshire Boulevard that K recalled she needed to buy a deodorant.

Of course, he did not take her to the nearest CVS, that wasn't Bill's style. He was probably really enjoying the ride, or maybe he just wanted to impress her with his knowledge of the hidden parts of town, but they ended up in a neighborhood he knew pretty well, where he used to get dope, many years before. She had no idea where she was, just off the main street, and she still couldn't understand why it was so hard to find what she was looking for, a simple antiperspirant roll-on. She would soon understand that Bill was not a normal human being.

He assumed that she had no idea what a Rite Aid was, being Italian. He turned the radio on and touched her leg, both to reassure and arouse her with the contingence of his skin.

"It's been a while since I came here," he said, "but I remember there's a place just around the block where you might find what you're looking for. Maybe not a fancy brand though. I hope you don't mind. But this way you can see the other side of Los Angeles."

K didn't really care about a deodorant brand, she was so nervous about being in the car with him. He pointed at Johnie's Coffee Shop on the corner of Wilshire and Fairfax. She did not know anything about it, and he wisely unfolded its story, from the very early fifties when the place opened its legendary doors and flashed the city of LA with its neon lights.

I was living in between Los Angeles and New York when Johnie's closed its legendary doors. So I never got the chance to actually have a meal in there. K actually did, a couple of days after the ride with Bill, by herself, for breakfast, while reading the morning news, and to feel his aura again, lost in the words of a *New York Times* with Clinton's smiling and reassuring face on the front page.

Listening to Bill talk was like listening to an underground history book. He had gotten into her brain before getting into her body.

Bill finally found the place he was looking for and pulled over into a small parking lot next to an old and shattered Mexican drug store. When K got back in, the only deodorant she could find was an old, most likely expired, Revlon Hi and Dry.

When she got back to the car, she did not feel like complaining. He had been nice enough to drive a stranger in rush hour to buy a beauty product. So she simply opened the bottle and asked him to smell it.

"Jesus, K! Is this really the only one you could find?" Bill asked laughing. "It smells like old lady powder. You sure this is OK?"

"I'm positive."

"But I like the name." He smiled. "See? That's the kind of Hollywood guy I am, taking a woman to a low-class neighborhood to buy beauty stuff."

"Well, I'm glad you're not," she said. "I probably wouldn't have had coffee and gone deodorant shopping with you. Let's say it's not the best fragrance. You should feel privileged, buying deodorant with a woman is some pretty intimate stuff..."

"Very intimate," he smiled. "Kind of post-coital without getting coital."

That's what made K fall in love. Bill was dark and troubled, but his humor was exactly what she was looking for. He gently touched her leg, again, with no evident sexual intention. He was a master at this game. And when she smiled at him, back on Wilshire, on the way to her hotel, they knew that day was just the beginning.

He pulled over across the street from the hotel and turned off the engine.

"Thank you for the beautiful day," K said. "It was fun."

"You are very welcome. My pleasure. I am going to Paris for a couple of weeks, but maybe we can have dinner sometimes, as soon as I get back."

"I'd love to."

"Enjoy Los Angeles."

She got off, trying to hide the sweetest and most embarrassing smile. Her heart raced and she was fifteen all over again. She crossed the street and looked at the Corvette leaving in the distance, in the heavy traffic of rush hour.

West to East with No Return

"The Weary Kind" by Ryan Bingham

When he came back from Europe, three weeks later, they met for what was supposed to be just another coffee. They decided on a windy and cloudy Saturday afternoon, right by the ocean at Shutters On the Beach.

This time K was anxious. She had been secretly waiting to see him again. After finishing an article for the new issue of one of the Italian fashion magazines she worked for, the dress-up process began: she wanted to be beautiful but, at the same time, not too dressed up for the occasion.

It was a peculiar circumstance, since she barely knew the real reason why they were seeing each other again. She did not know what Bill represented. A mentor, or a possible lover; probably simply an interesting man she had met during one of her first interviews. K genuinely had no idea, but she had that kind of jittery excitement of early love, that fear and sexual tension she had rarely experienced for a man without the help of drugs or alcohol. That's why she just wanted to enjoy the journey, no matter what the destination was, almost as if Bill were an experiment.

After a quick stop at the gas station, K drove her red Camaro to Santa Monica.

What the hell am I doing here? she thought, when she arrived at Shutters.

She sat on the bench outside near the beach track for a couple of minutes. She wrote a note in her purple diary. She felt alive, the ocean breeze blowing over her skin, and the emotion wildly scary, powerful, beautiful. Why did she ever need drugs if someone like Bill could make her feel that way?

The hotel was stunning in its beach-chic style—built the year before, in 1993, with the feel of a romantic grand resort hotel of the twenties; light shades of wood with elegant white terracing right on the Santa Monica beach. The architecture and its colors naturally blended with the surroundings. She felt warm, kissed by the beauty of something new and unexpectedly romantic. After a smoke, she carefully touched-up her lips and made her entrance into the luxurious lobby of the hotel.

K was not accustomed to this kind of elegance, but she appreciated Bill's idea of being by the beach.

He was waiting for me. And he was handsome. K wrote, failing to hide the vulnerability that her attraction brought on. *Bill had just that kind of charm that took my breath away. Dressed completely in black, wearing a leather jacket, he was waiting for me at the last table in the room, the one by the window, ocean view, drinking tea. Candles burned everywhere, but Bill shined out of his own darkness.*

I could feel it on my skin just reading K's words: fire. Just their hands touching burned. They talked and studied each other, though that tension did not let them actually concentrate on what either of them was saying. Bill knew how much she loved the ocean breeze, she had told him during the Canter's lunch, and he wanted her to feel it on her skin, to be comfortable for the evening ahead. In an almost uncanny way, they managed to cut the world out, all the people and their meaningless talk. They were alone and it felt like paradise.

The very first time everything was clear to me was when he casually, gently, and sensually caressed my face and my lips with his experienced hands. He terrified me somehow, and that's why I couldn't stop wanting him. The physical connection between us was established in that exact moment. The touch of our skin was an emotional orgasm we both felt. It was blood, flesh, and fire.

K stopped worrying and asking herself what would happen. Bill got up and unexpectedly kissed her on his way to the restroom. Without a word, he took her face into his hands and touched her lips with a romantic violence she had never experienced before.

Our tongues engaged in something beautiful and already addictive, K wrote. It was pure instinct. We just kissed, as it was the only possible step we could take from there. That was our first kiss.

For the first time in ages K felt comfortable in her own skin. When she was with him she wasn't scared of not being enough. She wasn't scared of not being perfect. Bill had the ability to make her feel just fine.

He was dope. He was food. He was every drug, and abstinence from it. Bill was heaven and hell braided together. He had it all, the whole package. And he shared it with me. He was the perfect drug.

Coffee was not enough, they wanted more. Still too early to have dinner, they just went for a walk on the beach. The sky was heavy with clouds and a breathtaking shade of silver had just melted into the cold ocean; a perfect fusion of metaphysical lights that they stared at for hours. They walked, slowly. They walked and studied each other's body movement, every single line, and every single muscle. They walked towards Malibu, but without a real destination.

When they returned to the restaurant their table was ready, on the terrace, absorbed in a soft and warm rainbow made of light wood, and creamy white walls, with candles everywhere and blue hydrangeas on each table.

Everything was going great, but K had not planned for after dinner. Once finished with the intimate meal of seafood and Italian white wine, for her, as he did not drink anymore, she didn't know what to do. A part of her was scared to death and simply wanted to end it there, before anything bigger could start. She thought about going her way and fantasizing about the night, alone in her bed. But then, Bill was still in front of her.

"What do you want, K?" He asked.

"What kind of question is that?" K replied, well aware of what he meant, but ignoring the uncomfortable conversation, not sure about the answer she wanted to give.

Bill caressed her lips with his fingers. He knew that she wanted something more than he was willing to offer.

Without thinking about the consequences, K decided to listen to her heart and not to her brain. Since Bill had parked at the hotel, he drove her back to the Santa Monica Pier parking lot, just a couple of minutes from there, where K's car was. She followed him home.

The drive was long. And she had no idea where the house was located, up the hills after at least three different freeways. K followed his car very carefully for almost fifty minutes, and her head did not stop for almost the entire ride. She found herself all the way east on the highest hill, in the opposite part of town, back in Los Angeles, in Echo Park. But when they finally arrived at his place, any tension she was feeling was immediately killed by the staggering view.

What attracted K the most to Bill was his badness, his mystery, and how he had redeemed himself, yet could not completely let go of his painful and tortured past. Bill had been married, but he had never been the relationship kind of guy. He had been a cheater most of his life, but even with such an addictive, rude, and passionate personality, women apparently could not say no to him. He was a solitary poet with a tormented soul, who was still struggling to find his way into the world. He was a man who had built his knowledge through pain, who lived in hell, and liked it more than heaven.

A Whole Package

Bill's beautiful house was far from the civilized world. It almost did not look like Los Angeles to K's eyes. The city flashed its glow from a distance, while gifting the beautiful terrace with a magical display of reflections, shades, and light. It created a painting of downtown LA with the dark sky above.

"I'm sorry that I don't have any wine," Bill said. "Would you like some tea?"

"It's okay. Tea is fine." She lit a cigarette while Bill put the water to boil in a pot and took care of Lila, his old black dog with a purple tongue. He had been gone for the whole day and the dog was acting crazy when he finally returned home with a not-so-unexpected guest.

Bill showed K the whole place, which was immense and stunning. In that artistic madhouse she could feel culture, a love for literature. She couldn't even count how many books he lived with. They were everywhere and she could smell them. The scent of Hemingway inebriated the rooms, and she couldn't help but notice how Bill was able to create art by just living in a secluded confusion of old movies, books, and records, within the confines of a fascinating and elegantly wild shelter. The black and white of the expensive jazz vintage photos on the walls gave a touch of New York to the almost Zen furniture. It was a balanced and careless fusion of East and West, tradition and modernity, all wrapped up in a cover of fine taste and what was left of the gutter he had lived in for too long. He did not have a microwave. Talk radio was always on.

"It's for a new book I am working on," he seemed to be justifying. "I hope it doesn't bother you."

"It doesn't. I can't wait to read it. How old is she?" K asked, petting Lila; the dog seemed to already be in love with her.

"You won't believe it, but she is seventeen," Bill said. "I rescued her from a shelter downtown four years ago when I was finishing my last novel. We've been walking together in the woods at night ever since. When you have a dog you feel like less of a creep walking in the woods at four in the morning."

"She's beautiful!"

"Do you want to come with us or you'd rather wait here? I really have to walk her for a while."

K touched his hand. "Of course I'm coming. Just let me grab my sweater."

"Take my jacket. It's freezing outside."

She quickly finished her cigarette. Bill had quit smoking years before and she did not want to bother him with her habit and the unpleasant smell. Whenever she was in his presence it felt like a blessing, the idea that such a man was even interested in a small town girl like K. She was afraid to ruin it, to break the link, the connection with a future she dreamed about.

"Wow, you are quite the whole package, huh?" Bill said, on their walk. K kept answering his questions about her life, how she had ended up in Los Angeles, lonely, and broken in pieces, on the edge of something, about to resurface. Bill was not naive. He had been there many years before. And K's aura both attracted and terrified him.

"That's what they say."

"Do you scare them?"

"They usually run away. I am too much of a burden, apparently, when they are not like me. You know what I mean..."

Bill took K's hand and put Lila's leash in it. Without knowing her at all, he could just feel the hurt. Bill was able to understand. And there was no judgment involved. Words were not necessary, but his eyes said it all.

After an hour of walking, they came back to the house. Tension grew rapidly. They were alone in the middle of nowhere. They wanted it and there was no reason for unnecessary denial. Everything started on the terrace, with downtown LA and Dodger Stadium at their feet. She hovered towards to him when his hand slowly and naturally found its way under her long dress.

It wasn't cold anymore.

He caressed my leg with a perfect touch made of desire, animal instinct, and selfish possession. He wanted me and his hands were about to take what was his for the night. My body surrendered and relaxed, and when his hand started moving slowly inside me, I knew there was no way back. We were in it together. The only thing I could think of, still on the terrace, while he was losing control, was that I needed him inside me. His hand was not enough anymore, although he knew I wanted his fingers to keep moving. I needed to feel his body slowly entering mine. I needed the slow and wild wave of blood to become stronger, intimate, devastating.

"You want this, baby, right?" Bill made sure I wanted it; one last time before it was too late. Maybe he just wanted me to beg for pleasure.

We craved it like the second scotch. We swam into a chill and humid air, and we created soft and curvy lines with our sweaty bodies and twisted minds. Our skin smelled an irresistible fragrance, sinful fairy tale; love. Bill was strong and violent at times; he hurt me and I was so scared and turned on by his touch that the only thing I could do was let go and become his loving slave. He was penetrating such an intimate part of me that it made no difference between his rough voice in my ears or the wild dance of his tongue on my lips, on my sex, my neck. His hands were choking me, and his teeth were biting my nipples until I almost cried, begging for relief. I felt my un-virgin skin penetrated by something exquisite and fierce. I couldn't control it, even if I wanted to. Bill knew what I liked. He knew what I was afraid of and what turned me on. Bill could read my mind and play with it. He tasted damn good, like dark cherries and black tea. I didn't need to get high. I felt like I was being initiated into something completely new, to a new form of life or a new form of death. That night, I felt like a virgin again. When he tied me up to his bed with some expensive black leather that he kept in his closet, he drained me from the old and created a complete new shape of a woman.

We both came, almost together.

We both fed on each other.

They talked, she told him everything. He didn't. They made love again. Their bodies just rested for a while, still insatiable and starving after each round. K could not remember the last time a night like that one had enlivened her senses. She could not remember the last time she felt such energy flowing into her veins, so much so that she felt the urge to reveal the one secret no one knew. K felt both the comfort and the urge to tell Bill something very important that had happened four years earlier and that completely changed her sexual life.

At first, she did try to impress him, barely covered by the dark blue sheets, still warm, with his hand reassuring her body. After all, he was a man who had tried it all, and his experience frightened her as much as sex in another language did. In a way, she believed that by sharing with him one of the most extreme and dramatic sexual experiences of her life, they would end up on the same level, that a shameful secret could make her more interesting to his eyes.

But she was barely a few words into the past, and everything changed. She started shivering and almost crying when revisiting her damaged and painful night, back in December 1990.

Only at the end of that long night would K realize why for all that time she had never allowed the truth to come out; she had never truly accepted it. The truth was that she had actually never forgiven herself. And she had spent years dispensing lies, before she had met Bill.

Bill listened to K's words. She turned her back to him and took him back to Italy, four years earlier.

Dogging-land: When Everything Changed

The iPod was OFF

DECEMBER 2, 1990. K and her former boyfriend, Marco, were hanging out at their usual club. They were drunk and she was high.

"I needed more," K whispered, knowing that Bill would never judge.

"We were making out in front everybody and even though it was not unusual for us, there was something different that night. I wanted more blow and we were crossing a line; he was very drunk. Marco pushed me into something more extreme to get the drugs, and I was so desperate that I would have said yes to anything he'd asked me."

K never understood to what extent she had started using sex to prove she had control over an old image she thought people had of her: of the fat girl from high school. Sex was a form of revenge most of the time, or just another narcotic. One day, without even being aware of it, she started surviving on the idea that sex was the only thing a man could desire from her. She was good at it and it empowered her.

From that moment, it had become a thankless job, something to push farther, beyond any imaginable limit, for love, of course. Love was always her excuse. It had become her weapon to keep men by her side, make them fall and surrender to a beauty she could not see in the mirror—a connecting link between their souls. K had become the sex girl, for a dose of love she was desperate to get, and couldn't find anywhere else.

Before then, she had experimented with a threesome and a stripper, then sex with another couple. But the new frontier was having sex with her boyfriend in front of a live audience that was masturbating and making specific requests. In writing, she remembered how much they all loved the shape of her lips, when she stayed down on her knees, submissive, a martyr for love. She also recalled how much they liked her fetish lingerie and the extreme strip tease she gifted them with. K needed to be in the spotlight when she was high, and since Marco's eyes were not ever exclusively on her, she needed other men to be hypnotized by her skills.

They blow lines from my skin, they lick it from me and the bitter tastes better with the sweat of the effort I put into being perfect at what I do. I keep snorting when they are inside me. I don't even care who they are, as long as I feel the rush. I feel beautiful. When I wake up in the morning, a ghost, I just do it again and again. The pain goes away and I disappear. I am somebody else, thin and powerful. That's not me. And as long as it isn't me, I can keep going forever.

She was high that night and so drunk that she would have done anything to get more cocaine. Nevertheless, she lacked the money for even a gram. That's what tricked her into the labyrinth. In the relationship with Marco, K always played the weak part. Being the victim was her profession. So much so that the feeling of self-pity became her field of expertise, something she could proudly claim on her résumé right after BA in Foreign Languages and Literatures. But she was also in love; she would have done anything for him. And he knew it.

Marco never did drugs. He was an old-fashioned alcoholic. He was a good man, but he was in pain, too. They both had no path to follow and bonded to feel warm again, loved again. He was just destroying himself with a woman like K, who lacked self-respect and self-love. Although there was a time he cared for her, she could not recall how it felt.

"Marco didn't like my little cocaine secret, which wasn't really a secret any more," K continued.

In fact, he had nothing against the chemical realm, quite often tripping himself on Xanax and Scotch to forget the heavy hurt of existence they had been both destined to suffer since the early days of motherly womb.

"He wasn't concerned about my health," she said, "but he had always considered doing blow an awfully rich gesture. And heroin was not his cup of tea; I guess he didn't like needles. But the snorting thing was disgusting according to his political and philosophical takes on life. But that night he wanted his sex fantasy to become a reality. He didn't care about what I would do to say yes."

K looked down at her naked body, covered by Bill's blue sheets.

"He wanted to see his girlfriend being fucked by another man. He wanted to see the guy coming on my skin, on my red lips, with my tongue finishing it all, until I'd swallow every last drop. Marco was very determined. He was dying to jerk off while watching me, scared, with my legs wide open for the strangers in line at the street corner, where the park downtown opens to the public.

"He would slowly take my clothes off and guide my hand, for the show to start. Like I didn't know how to touch myself. What I would get in return was not his business when he was drunk. A blowjob for a fix on the street? That was a deal to him. If that was all I needed to be his whore, getting loaded and saying yes, it was fine, just for that night.

"The day after he would hate himself for going that far. But that night, scotch and sex screamed louder than heart."

That is exactly what they did, at first. They drove around from one dealer to another, on a freezing and humid street in a bad neighborhood. The deal was pretty simple: her mouth for half a gram, her body for a bag, and with two men the discussion was open for something more.

A beautiful, young, scared woman selling herself for dope, with her boyfriend right there to watch and manually enjoy the show: is there anything more damaged and pathetic?

K sat on the passenger side, when the first yes walked closer to the car, hovering down to examine the wares, and she started shaking. She wanted to throw up. She wanted to seal the deal and shoot her fix right there. At least the whole thing would have had a purpose, but when the tall Senegalese man touched her leg through the front window to examine the goods for sale, she just couldn't do it. Not for the drugs.

I'm not a fucking junkie, she remembered thinking in the last moment of sanity. *I can't, babe. Let's do it without it. I just need another beer.*

Back in the room with Bill, K looked at him and he sweetly kissed her shoulder. She took a deep breath and went back to Italy, again.

She did not do it for the drugs that night. She did it for love. Just by closing her eyes she could still recall his smell…

"It was cheap cologne, way too much," she said, while Bill silently felt her shame.

"The man was in his early fifties. And his hair was freshly washed with some buy-one-get-one-free discount shampoo. But it was clean, at least. That penetrating and dry perfume was the perfect anesthetic to help me concentrate on something else while his sweaty and uncomfortable body pushed against mine, trying to make its way where it didn't belong. That's how I started the first erotic show for the man I thought was the love of my life, by ignoring the voice inside my head.

"It was the coldest winter I could remember, but I was wearing thigh-high boots with a silky, black minidress that barely covered me. In my mind, at that time, a man wouldn't love a woman like me in jeans and a T-shirt. And I just couldn't afford to lose the only thing I could offer to Marco...you know, I am not stupid..." she laughed, to hide the tears. "I was well aware that my only weapons with him were my body, sex, and always saying yes. We were fucked up."

"What did you get in exchange?" Bill asked.

"A couple of hours of fake love, when alcohol was running in his veins, and protection in his arms, before he sold me out to reach his open-air orgasm. A kiss of gratitude and approval when everything was done. I just wanted to make love to him. But let me continue or I'll change my mind."

"Of course, I'm sorry," Bill apologized, running his fingers through her hair. He was intrigued by the story, but nonetheless felt for K's unresolved guilt.

"I drank my double malt beer in the freezing car. I had lost count of them already. I was still high, and I wasn't really cold even though it was winter. We parked where everything was supposed to happen. Two a.m. on an early December night. Silence. The place was mystical with the old castle right before us, a beautiful monument from the Middle Ages. It made the whole place look like a set for some kind of Hollywood historical flick.

"You know, I never quite understood why such a cultural place was the meeting point for men and women that didn't get enough of their own partners, yet there I was, right next to my love and scared to death."

K was about to lose it all that night. She was about to lose her second virginity and she was about to let the guilt of a secret and unwanted pleasure change her life forever.

"Barely five minutes had passed; Marco could not wait, like a child on Christmas morning. He started playing with my skirt and when he made me show an inch of skin, reassuring me that everything was fine with his gentle, yet lustful hand, forty or maybe fifty masturbating hunters came out of the bushes, looking for their prey. They were trying to impress me with their abilities, eager to catch my attention with their erections. I was the cause, but I wasn't even trying to turn them on. I shivered at their sight. Thank God I was so high. I played with the silk of my skirt and I started to touch my legs. I know how to touch myself, but there was something wrong about it and even if I was fucked up I knew it was bad. That's why, after five minutes, I hesitated and I told him I wanted to go home. I had changed my mind.

"We were still in the park but already driving towards the exit gate when I got so scared of losing and disappointing him that I touched his leg to stop the car. I chose our man, as four had followed us, Marco driving very slow, perhaps hoping. In that exact moment I looked into his eyes and never saw his pride and satisfaction. I thought I was doing the right thing. That's the last

conscious decision I made, before it all began just around
the corner. From that moment, I let him direct the game.
I actually let them both decide every single move, because
I was there to please. I could barely move; I was terrified.

"Everything began so quickly that I didn't even have
time to kiss him. God! Can you believe it?"

"Why?" Bill asked.

"Because he was already taking photos of the two of
us, with his new camera. It's called dogging and it's all the
rage in Europe.

"While watching his woman being violated by a
stranger," she continued, not scared anymore, but almost
turned on by the guilty memory and ashamed of it, "he
had to take pictures and masturbate, enjoying the show.
I was the show. Isn't that what every girl wants? Fifteen
minutes of fame? Smile, you're on camera?

"So, the stranger opened my legs and he took what
was his for the night; his fingers were already inside
me. Maybe I was just high, maybe it was my boyfriend
masturbating in front of me and telling me how beautiful
I was, but after a couple of minutes I found myself wet,
and fighting the unwanted pleasure. I was so ashamed that
I stopped his hand and took control. On my knees I did
my job; I was the pleasure giver, after all. But they wanted
more and I had to let go.

"Marco told us what he wanted to see, according to
him we were actors on a set and he was directing the show.
He had the last word and those innocent games were not
what he had signed up for. He wanted sex. He wanted me

brutally fucked. And, for as much as I hate to say it, at that point, I was so turned on that a part of me wanted it, too. I felt so dirty, and at the same time I was exploding, I needed to come. There was a war in my brain; there was a war between my legs."

It went on for more than an hour. She tried so hard not to enjoy it that the man inside her could sense her fear, the contracted muscles and her attempt to destroy the guilty pleasure. He was gentle and nice yet still a stranger K didn't want in her body, still a foreigner in her heart.

"There's no fucking heart involved." K reminded herself.

The only pathetic reason why she was letting him tear her veil was just to make her man proud; it was just to make him love her, once and for all.

If you have lived long enough to know, you acknowledge that it does not work that way—love, I mean. You don't have to humiliate yourself, bleeding on your knees in a park, covered with icy and glittery snow, when the only thing you need is a kiss without a price.

"The stranger stood before me," she continued, "and I was on a cold iron bench, legs wide open in a pathetic effort at being perfect in Marco's eyes. The swirling dress I was wearing was so short that it was like being completely naked. I felt powerful, even though I knew I was the slave. In my sick and weak mind, my legs prevented him from running away. My sex inebriated him and because I had that kind of power everything would be just fine. How ridiculous and pathetic.

"My thong was dark purple lace and it covered such a small inch of skin that I'm sure the stranger did not even notice it. Paolo was his name. I always pay attention to the details. I should have known that my dealer was screwing with me," she laughed, drugs did not delete that memory as she had hoped. He wanted it so bad that he couldn't resist the temptation of a scared first-time girl. It must have been the perfect night for him. I was the sacrifice; I was the lamb and he wanted more and more. His hands almost hurt me, and he was not even human anymore, but a hungry beast instead. My body was at his disposal, every inch of flesh. He could do whatever he wanted, and he did.

"I remember the stranger telling me that he wanted to hear my voice and that's when I started whispering. He needed to hear my scared voice in his ears and that's when I started coming. My boyfriend wanted more, too, until they got it all. Nothing was left of me. I came, as ashamed as I had ever been in my entire life. Paolo did, too. Every single drop on my cherry Chanel-colored lips."

K took a deep breath.

"The morning after, I wanted to die. I got up and he was still asleep. So I showered three times to wash away my sins. It didn't work.

"I thought about calling Melissa, my best friend. But she would have judged me, and I was already judging myself enough. So, I kept the secret and tried to delete every single frame that brought back to memory the night in the park from my mind. I looked at myself in the mirror and I had never hated my body so much, not even when

I was fat and mocked by my classmates. I got dressed in a long T-shirt of his and I put my black coat on. I grabbed my high-heeled boots, reached for the purse and left him a smoke on the kitchen table. He was still sleeping when I silently left."

Bill and K fell asleep with the sun almost rising and fighting the thick clouds of the early Los Angeles morning. He kissed her and put his arm around her waist, almost to protect what was created earlier. They fell asleep watching the city waking up.

After her night with Bill, I found this letter, which she apparently wrote after sharing, about the night in the park. Maybe it was her way to finally close that chapter, after revealing the truth, or maybe writing was simply her sanity.

I've changed. You never did, and you never will.

The living proof of it is that guilt is killing me.

I had to let you behind; you would never follow me, if not down, in an early grave.

I know I will never feed on our open-air nights again and it won't snow like it like it did for us on Christmas day, many years ago.

Months have passed, and summer bothered our lovely, fake picture-perfect devastation.

Months have passed, but stayed in the same old place.

I was wearing my short electric-blue dress and tasted like salt and Tequila.

Few were the last remaining clients on the floor of the nightclub, the one in the city park, where sober was not an option for us.

I will never forget that night.

My hair was curly for the first time in years and no matter how much whiskey was flowing into your veins, cocaine in mine, you noticed it from the other side of the counter where I stood, smiling at you, tired.

You liked it. At 4:00 a.m. when you arrived, walking fearless with your casual black hair all sweaty from the humid summer air outside.

You were still with her, but that night I fell in love with you all over again.

And that was long before making love in the park,

Still drunk from the heavy metal screaming from inside the old asylum turned into a bar.

We didn't care; we just wanted each other.

The room was empty so we danced, for the first time since we had met.

Our private DJ played our favorite song.

I think it was The Cure or Adriano Celentano.

I can still breathe your skin, drunk with nicotine.

Your eyes were not sad for once, not like in the morning, I mean.

When I was almost too scared to exist in the charm of your apartment.

That night I washed away my memories to let you in again. And again, and again.

I wasn't afraid, my heart raced, and you were my fix. Sweetest injection, a hopeless perfection.

The only destruction I could allow from the outside.

We danced, and you made me feel beautiful.

We danced alone until sunrise.

Only then we sat outside with our beer, it wasn't dark any more,

And you finally kissed me.

It was time to go home.

I wanted that night to last forever,

Because our afternoon-morning was about to come;

And I was about to become your unbearable presence again.

That's why I left when you were still asleep.

I couldn't stand how much you hated me for being in your bed.

So I kissed you in your sleep,

You reached for my hand, not strong enough to keep me there.

I drove back home with tears in my eyes, like every weekend,

But then I convinced myself that the night would come again, and so would I, for another dose of my favorite pain.

I've changed. You never did, and you never will.

The living proof of it is that guilt is killing me, a thousand miles from there.

"A Pain That I'm Used To" by Depeche Mode

THE DAY AFTER, SHE left Bill's place at ten in the morning because he was speaking at a recovery center. She could sense that Bill did not want her there when he woke up. He made coffee. She drove home as fast as she could, her only wish to fall asleep and disappear, dead to the world.

"What do you want, K?" he had asked her over dinner the night before in Santa Monica. She knew. It was déjà-vu all over again and everything was crystal clear from the way he distractedly kissed her while giving her directions on how to take the freeway back to the west side. She felt it deep inside, she had let herself go, and now she was completely alone and lost. She had just shared with him one of her most painful secrets, and Bill was already gone, no matter how perfect and intense the night before had been.

Everything looks perfect from the highest mountain of Los Angeles. Everything looks perfect from far away.

A quote from K's diary reads, from the day that followed her night with Bill. She wrote it with a black marker, not her usual ballpoint.

Apart from too much Xanax and some stolen codeine, K was still trying to stay clean in those early Los Angeles days when she had just met Bill.

The first thing she went for, of course, was food. She poured herself a vodka with no ice for the Xanax to work faster, but she needed to fill the emotional disappointment in some hurtful way, and one of her favorite drugs happened to be a couple of blocks away from the apartment. It was legal and not even expensive.

Almost 7:00 p.m. There was no food in the apartment. The obsessive and violent voice in her head screamed and she couldn't help but listen. In that moment, angry with him, and with herself for being so naive, just like a drunk, she needed another glass. And she did not have any support there to pull her back from the ledge. She was going to have to save herself.

But she was blaming Bill and she already regretted the night they spent together. If there was something she was good at, it had always been blaming others for the choices she made. K wouldn't have asked him to help for anything in the world. She would have rather died.

Her veins almost tasted it; her mouth was dry and noxious because of the amount of nicotine and coffee she had had that day. Her hands were shaking like she was in withdrawal; she was sweating dirt, like when you get the wrong shit. Her whole body was trembling and trying to resist another failure. She needed to satiate the emotional hunger with every imaginable food: cream cheese frosting and pizza, bread and butter, strawberry cheesecake ice cream and cinnamon bread, milk and cornflakes and frosting again, bagels, croissants with butter and chocolate frosting, then milk again, for the liquid part to do its job when flushing it all away. Only then she would start the punishment, until finally bleeding and feeling clean, pure again.

When she was in this state, she could not control her thoughts, her words, her movements, her actions and impulses. The urge was so strong that it prevented her brain from focusing on anything else. K was deliberately choosing to listen to the voice. She consciously let it in, little by little.

She took two more Xanax and drank another vodka. Another Xanax and she finally felt better, relaxed, at least. Her body finally feeling lighter, the weight of pain lifting away, the voice whispering instead of screaming, her heart beating slower and slower in her chest.

She knew how it all worked. She did had done it for years, and she felt safe after yesterday, following the same old pattern to deal with life and emotions. She was not ready for what Bill had awakened in her.

Slowly fading away on her broken bed, the purging crisis no longer an emergency, K thought about her father again. The unsaid words, the unjustified hate.

K's father is a good-hearted man who truly loved his daughter; he would have done anything in his power to protect and to help her. For years he was terrified of showing that. He suffered deeply in seeing his own K slowly and deliberately hurting, but at the same time, I think that he felt powerless and afraid of facing this obstacle in their relationship.

K was in search of love, but she didn't even know what love truly was. When real love was offered to her, she ran from it. She wasn't able to love a mother and a father who, despite the mistakes they may have made, did love their daughter. K did not know how to deal with the reassuring warmth of a fatherly embrace. She hated it, and facing the wary love in his eyes was uncomfortable.

"I can't be in his arms," K told Dr. Carmen, choked by a disgraceful shame she had never felt before. "He tries to come closer, but I can't face him. The emotional discomfort becomes aversion, a physical reaction; does it make any sense? What kind of person am I? My father needs my love and I need to run away. The moment he wants me in his arms is when I need drugs, to escape constraint. I hate myself for doing this, and I don't know where it comes from but it's choking me, and I need it at the same time. I can't look him in the eyes. I feel so guilty. They're better off without me, at this point."

"Go on, K," Dr. Carmen said. "Let it all out."

"Do you remember when I told you I don't care about how my mother feels?" K continued. "Do you remember when I told you I don't care if she dies? That I hate her when she throws up and I can hear it from my bedroom? It was my disease. It was the only thing that was finally setting us apart, as two different women. I feel like she ripped me off and now I'm getting fatter and more disgusting as we speak. I fantasize about their deaths and I am afraid I won't feel any pain, but relief. What the fuck is wrong with me?

"I dream about their funeral. I can see myself, in the spotlight, with people that I don't even like suddenly paying attention to me. Even the priest I barely know is there; I am crying in the church, and everybody is comforting me. Is that what it takes? Do I really need to see them dead? I keep blaming them, but I am as guilty as they are. They taught me the difference between right and wrong and I don't know where the truth is anymore.

"Shame is the only thing that's left and I don't know where to go from here.

"You really want to know what it feels like to be disgusted when a father cries tears of joy when his daughter makes him proud? You want to know what it really feels like when they try to get close to me, and I just wish they were six feet under? I need the grief and not their care anymore. You questioned my sex life, many times," K said to the doctor. "Now I can give you the answer: It fills the emptiness inside for as long as I want it to. It gives me a dose of detached love that doesn't require emotional involvement. I give them what they want, they pretend they love me for a couple of hours and I feel like a queen. And, the morning after I can go back to life, where no one will ever touch me again until I let them."

This conversation took place a couple of years before moving to Los Angeles, and K remembered every single word. She didn't get any answer from Dr. Carmen, but according to the psychoanalytic big book, sharing was the key. Things did not change after the confession, but for the first time in her entire life she had admitted the crime, and some kind of relief, a lightness of spirit was the reward.

Life Without

"A Forest" by The Cure

Rain came down on Monday afternoon. That's how she started her diary that day, a couple of weeks since the night with Bill. Los Angeles was crying lonely, dusty tears of rain.

Not that she wasn't used to rainy weather, given her upbringing in the Alps and her years in London. She loved the smell and the sound of the rain in Hyde Park. The shapeless humid drops were part of the city, something that you either loved or hated. In Los Angeles, rain was different and hardly contemplated. London was beautiful in its white and gray shades, and mysterious when touched by the drops of its windy and dense rain.

The ocean can be melancholic and romantic with rainy, gusty weather, but Los Angeles itself is not. Its architecture was not meant for that kind of weather. Los

Angeles was built for the burning sun, for clouds, for
the Santa Ana winds, and the fires, but not for rain on a
Monday morning.

K had always been affected by the weather. They had
a love-hate relationship and that day, she hated it. The
drizzle and its smell as it evaporated from the broken
asphalt on La Cienega made her feel tired and weak, blue
and without life. It was not the right day to rain. Bill had
not yet called. Maybe she did not want him to. She was not
supposed to deal with a man in her life at that stage, she
was supposed to get sober and do yoga, drink more green
tea, and write a book.

For years I've been reading K's diary, debating on
how to tell her story. I respect and understand her feelings,
the disease; but at times, especially at the beginning of my
reading, I couldn't understand what she was looking for,
and why it was so hard for her to see the truth, pay attention
to that wake up call that had been ringing for her.

I don't know if she really loved him or if she was just
looking for someone else to hate, to fight, to blame, to
become addicted to. I don't know if she wanted Bill to
become an alternative to what she was about to choose.
I don't know what was K looking for in those early days.

Love was the least of her worries in that moment. She
had a deadline and she had to fight major cravings. She
needed to find a way out of her brain for the next hour or
so. She had an article to deliver, and since the interview
turned out to be more interesting than she had imagined,
work stopped her for a short while. But the cravings got

stronger. She started shaking and having cold sweats again; she walked in and out of the apartment five times with cash and cigarettes in her hand. It kept growing and she couldn't stop it, but she didn't want to do that to her body again. She stopped thinking straight; her brain became completely absorbed in that feeling of nonentity. She knew what she wanted and she wanted it so bad that her body was just waiting for its dose.

Cigarettes and vodka did not work. She took her Xanax and drank some water. She didn't have drugs at home or connections in town, barely enough money for a couple of hours of narcotic relief from the few codeine left, the ones she had stolen from a friend. She filled her body with water until it hurt so bad she couldn't even stand up straight: water, another vodka, cigarettes; water, another vodka, cigarettes; water, another vodka, cigarettes. She took her Xanax again. She wasn't high enough, and the plan didn't work as it was supposed to; her stomach hurt, but she still needed it, filling and emptying, filling and emptying, a never-ending story.

She just needed her dose; she just needed to kill the voice and feel full—she would then clean the body the only way she knew. She wanted someone to be there to help her, but no one magically appeared.

Help! She silently started screaming. *Someone fucking help me, please!* Red eyes and tears, tears of madness, tears of shame, tears of unspoken pain that she was still hiding, tears of hopelessness, and tears of repressed anger.

"I want to die!" She really screamed then, not caring if the neighbors could hear her. "Do me a favor, I failed to kill myself last time, I see this scar every fucking morning," she said looking at her right wrist, "but I'm still breathing, and the bleeding stopped. God, please, I fucking want to die; I'm begging you, for once in my life listen to me. Kill me!"

She was exhausted, and time drizzled, painfully slow. In one hour she would be safe; Carrie would come home from work and it would be too late to do it. She didn't want her to know. Not so early, at least.

She craved it like a dope fiend in downtown LA, selling the last penny to V., who would spit the happy balloon of Mexican tar in your hand, and you would welcome it like water in the desert. It was the key to paradise for the next few hours to come. Money can buy some happiness, wrapped up in a colorful balloon.

Her stomach hurt. Her head hurt. Her soul was devastated and weak. She could barely walk, and when she went back into her bedroom, she started to violently scrape her skin with her fingernails.

God, help me resist, please. If I don't die, help me get through it. I can't do that again. Please, don't let me do this now. Please, help me. I need help!

She took more Xanax and finally fell asleep, still crying.

When K woke up, in the middle of the night, Carrie was already asleep. She wrote a page in her diary but then decided to give her brain a rest and her body a place to lie down before starting all over again. She went back to bed and immediately fell asleep again. For that night at least, she was done with words and war.

"Roads" by Portishead

WHEN I DECIDED TO talk about K's life, I wanted to weave her journey into a smooth story, accessible while remaining authentic to the truth. When I found this letter in her diary, the only option I had was typing it exactly the way she wrote it, still with tears in my eyes. I truly believe I owe it to her:

Letter from K's diary, dated July 2nd

THERE ARE DAYS WHEN I'm stuck in thoughts that are bigger than me.

In those days, my own prison is a labyrinth in the past, and I cross the bridge of an old mistake again. I cut the line of misery. I can barely move.

I don't dream about a future, but make love to an old scar, written on my wrist, with some Chinese proverb that was supposed to remind me of my courage, of my strength when I was nineteen. Just another lie.

There are days when I lose control, and with it the perception of what I am.

It wasn't high school, I told them. But insanity, just giving birth to another form of me; my brain is so crowded.

I lost touch; I don't want to wake up anymore. Why should I be alive?

I feel full and empty at the same time, and I can't find the way out of a past that is slowly and dangerously becoming my present and future. But I want this; I don't know who I am without it.

I am stuck in between.

I hate what I am so much that I just wish there was a way to clear it all. No memories. I'd be willing to lose the very few good ones that I have.

No memories.

Looking back...I can see how much I lived. I see myself licking pills off a bathroom floor. My tongue tastes the painless vision and I sweat the regret for doing it; my mind isn't free.

Why does everything keep changing while my brain does not?

What's your plan, God? What's my part in all this? Is there really a purpose? Why am I still here? Why is the journey so lonely? Why has everything in my life ended? What was the purpose of living it then?

If a master plan does exist, this would be the right time for a hint.

Am I so blind that I cannot see it?

Three days, resting bones and the humid sand. Let the sun kiss me—let the sun warm my body.

Let something move, let something change—I can't do this any longer.

I need a light. I cannot drive the dark through.

Three days when the only thing I can do is cry, at least the pain leaves my skin untouched.

A prayer. The last thing I would have imagined doing, the last thing I wanted to try, but the last hope I have, to survive.

The thing is, my dear, the journey to hell, when you choose to walk that path, is very easy to reach. It's downhill.

It doesn't require a lot of effort when you just want to die.

But you can't walk that road forever.

When you realize it, you have a choice: you can die right there, in hell,

Or, you can live, true life.

And right there, when you find yourself crossing the bridge, the crossroad of your entire life, you know what true hell really is.

The hardest part has just begun.

You won't have your favorite self-harming weapons this time.

You won't have easy escapes.

The only thing you're going to have is a wounded self, someone you have always despised and resented. Someone you have tried to destroy throughout your entire life.

That's why I am crying like a child.

And I am praying for help.

I'm just praying for someone above to give me his hand; to help me walk out of hell.

I pray, and pray. Like I never did before.

Reading more about her, I found out she wrote that letter while in Venice Beach, on a summer afternoon. It was July 9, 1994, three months after the night at Bill's, five months after Kurt Cobain had been found dead in his

Seattle home. This death had devastated her, so much so that instead of realizing she could follow Kurt sooner than she wished, she had followed the blond guy around the corner, where tourists do not adventure, where what you pay for is exactly what you get.

Early the next morning, after the shy tanning day on the beach, K went downstairs to pick up the mail, still with coffee and cigarette in her hands. At first, nothing seemed different from what she would always find: utilities to pay, a letter from the bank offering a new deal for an additional credit card, a quote from an insurance company, and then a surprise: an elegant black envelope, with a stamp from Los Angeles sent two days before.

It's Just a Letter

"Country Feedback" by R.E.M.

To the rest of the world, K was doing fine. She knew how to make new friends when she wanted to, and no one knew that she had slowly started using again. Mostly cocaine in those days, the drug that took everything away from her, and that was easier to get through those few contacts she already had in town. Her blond Venice Beach friend had suddenly disappeared and she didn't know where to get heroin, other than from him. It wasn't easy for an Italian girl, still scared by the Los Angeles drug scene, to jump into it with no reservations. Fear wouldn't last long for K, but codeine and cocaine were fine. She was not planning on going back to her old life anyway. Just a temporary help, that's how she would justify it in front of the bathroom mirror that never lied.

Her anxiety and panic attacks were sedated by a daily side dish of Xanax, and everything looked just fine from the outside. K naively thought she had things under control.

She was finally getting used to her new life. She had made some new friends, was writing a lot, and managing to make her connections work. She wasn't happy, but she was at least becoming artificially less unhappy. That is how she liked to define her condition, when someone asked her how she was doing, omitting the "artificial."

K really thought she had found a balance between insanity and a normal life among people in the real world. She thought of herself as a gloomy, solitary artist that needed the drugs and the pain to create. She had adhered to the cliché, and did not need, nor want, any true success, because usually, when she was about to reach the top, she would deliberately fall for fear of failing.

She always believed in a black or white view of the world. K had never been able to admire and embrace any shade of gray. It was either good or bad, yin or yang, heaven or hell, all or nothing. She still believed in that kind of a vision, but she had started to accept the human condition. She got to a point where she understood that in order to survive she had to make a compromise with her mind, whether she liked it or not. She made the conscious choice to take some part-time drugs to help her cope, not to party and have fun, just to feel normal, control the hunger and deal with the terms of life.

K kept holding the envelope in her hands. She lit another cigarette and poured some more coffee in her mug, with that tiny bit of milk that made the perfect combination of creamy and bitter.

I need a shot of Scotch to open it, she thought.

It would have been more powerful than a cup of coffee, but she was still trying to be off alcohol in the morning, and scotch for breakfast, just to open a letter, wasn't part of the plan. She was following a very strict set of rules in order to work, she was entitled to only a couple of lines of cocaine or some codeine to get her through the assignments. Alcohol and Xanax were for the night, an early one, so that she could wake up early in the morning and write the news for Italy, which was nine hours ahead.

It's just a stupid letter, she moved it around, like a snow globe. *Another fashion show I have to go to for a stupid magazine. I'd go if they would fucking pay me.*

She did not yet know many people in town and the few friends she had were not sending letters. She had no idea who could have sent her such an invite at her home address.

Why can't I just read it and toss it? I'm being ridiculous. She kept playing with it, while looking at the cigarette butts and the orange peels in the trashcan. *I'll open it at the count of three.*

K slowly touched the elegant lines of the letter with her burgundy fingernails, like that gesture could be of any help in identifying the sender. Deep inside she already knew, or maybe she was just secretly hoping, that Bill would come back. Her heart raced again, just like on the beach of Santa Monica, four months earlier, while waiting to meet the old and mysterious man that had stolen her heart and made it his on a windy Saturday afternoon.

She had not heard from Bill in quite a long time and she had gotten to the point where it was better that way. K had thought about the whole situation thoroughly; he was way too old and fucked up, certainly not the kind of man she needed in her life. Particularly if she had to beg for his presence. After the first initial disappointment, she had managed to stop thinking about it, since nothing had actually happened, apart from an intense night together.

He fed my lips with a pulpy pear. He cut it with an old knife and gently let my faltering mouth grab it from his hands. He fed me forbidden fruit and careless care. But we just had fun. It is okay for it to be over. She wrote to finally end the Bill chapter in her diary.

After the fourth smoke, K finally opened the black envelope and her world fell apart in a second.

I know we haven't talked in ages, and I am sorry for that, but I would love to see you again. I am signing my new book on Sunday night. It's at the Chateau Marmont, 8221 Sunset Blvd. 7:30 p.m.
I was really an asshole to let you go the way I did.
Just think about it and you'll make an old man happy.
—Bill

She debated whether she really wanted to read those words, and whether she wanted Bill to come back. She had put the memory of the adventure with him in the past, something to remember and to forget. She hated him that morning, but she couldn't stop reading the letter and thinking of the terrace, his voice, his bed, and the blue sheets.

Wake up K, she thought. *This is LA. The only thing a man wants from you is sex, especially if he is thirty years older than you.*

She finished her coffee, got dressed, and headed to a meeting with her boss at the press agency. The head office was based in the Hollywood Hills, but that morning they were meeting for breakfast in Westwood, before heading to a press junket together in a hotel nearby. The letter remained on the coffee table, exactly where she had read it, covered by a trail of silvery ash accidentally dropped from her last smoke before heading to the car, parked one block away on dirty Guthrie Ave.

While driving on Wilshire Boulevard, she could not stop thinking how stupid she'd be in even considering the idea of attending the book signing to see Bill again. She was wasting time and energy just in using her brain—or heart, if she was being honest—to even think about it instead of focusing on how to save money for writing classes or to buy a new car, since the red Chevy Camaro a friend gave her was in constant need of expensive maintenance, and she would have to return it sooner or later, anyway.

It was cold and the rain fell poorly yet still gave no sings of halting. The smell reminded her of sweet Septembers in London a few years before. She loved walking by Liverpool Street Station. The memories of East London and Ealing Broadway, blurred by drugs.

She couldn't forget the big concert in Trafalgar Square, and saying yes to everything some guy had to offer, after meeting him across the street from the South African Embassy.

It had gotten colder and the rain had started pouring down. The only color that stood out that morning was her red lipstick. The drive took particularly long. The elegance of Beverly Hills saddened her, especially when she stopped at a red light across the street from the Beverly Wilshire Hotel, where she had met Bill for the very first time.

The letter was wearing on her and in trying to find an alternative to losing it entirely, K consciously decided to let her demons slip back in. Life was too complicated.

The disgust she felt for her own body prevented her from even handling the easiest evening tasks. She wasn't able to shower. She could not bear the existence of her naked body. Its reflection in the mirror was too much to acknowledge and respect. She had bought that mirror with Carrie at a garage sale in Pasadena while shopping for cocaine and weed. She couldn't let the warm water of the bath touch her skin, which she felt was thick and infected. K just wanted to melt it in fire, like an old, useless iron tool. Bill's words were not working, she was writing but it was not turning all around.

The symptoms came back again. Her fragile hope faded away day after day, hour after hour, minute after minute.

"Right Where It Belongs" by Nine Inch Nails

As USUAL, SHE WASHED the dishes and the coffee cup from earlier in the morning. The only food she had for dinner was a rice cake with cream cheese, but she went through the whole cleaning process to feel like she had a regular, pleasant meal. K liked to feel like a normal person some days, the part of the world that watched the news and had a burger and fries with friends.

After finishing up at the sink, K poured herself some cheap CVS vodka, lit a cigarette, and sat on the couch.

"You are not supposed to mix it with Xanax, or whatever you are taking. You know that, right?" Carrie asked as she walked past the couch, glancing at her.

"It's just a glass. It's been a long day and I need to sleep," she justified.

She had started to drink more and more every day. But it had been too long since she had last had a decent sleep in her bed, not on the couch for a couple of hours before dawn. The screaming inside had become unbearable. She made sure Carrie wasn't anywhere near and stole some of her leftover weed from the night before, after which she silenced the TV and finally went into her bedroom. Not caring about the growing pile of clothes covering the bed, she turned on Conan and closed her eyes.

K was used to a wide array of chemical alterations, but that night, the migraine was too heavy to sustain. It felt like her brain was about to burst and disintegrate. It was not a regular headache. It was a cry for help—a scream from within, begging her to stop.

With her eyes closed, K wished for anyone else's brain, maybe even Bill's. She envied his pain, his struggle, and his damage.

The truth is that she always envied other people's happiness in the daylight, but when the night came, she envied other people's pain, too.

His burden was somehow more attractive, easier to handle, because he seemed not to care—and to K that was the cure: stop caring, stop feeling. She was not sure about the nature of the war inside his own mind, she knew he suffered and yet Bill had only showed her indifference. That letter was just more confusing and unnecessarily brought him back to mind.

K wished she were Bill, just for one night. She thought of him, trying to write in his house. She missed his books and how safe she had felt in his living room. She missed the dark luxury of his bedroom. She longed for the smell of his leather jacket, his hands, and how he managed to hide his feelings.

How did you learn? She asked, almost ashamed of such a pointless question.

Why didn't you tell me how to do it? That's the only thing I needed from you, your experience in the art of pretending. I begged for your sober anesthetizing recipe, I never asked you to save me. But just to teach me how to be you. For you have survived.

She fell in love with him at first sight. She had fallen in love with him when he approached her at the press conference and read the pain in-between the lines of her scars. But in those three months apart, she had also realized that nothing would come out of it.

She couldn't stop thinking about the slow and precise movement of his hand, making its way under her dress, the very first night on the terrace. She wanted him inside her more than anything else. She would never forget how terrified she was while pushing her body against his, hard and beautifully dangerous. His hands couldn't stop, neither could her thirsty mouth, moisturizing his chest with her tongue, and slowly lowering down, onto her knees to swallow his pleasure for the night. She wanted him.

I want to feel your lonely nights; I need you to take my pain away, she said, while picturing him in a crowded bed. *I need to know how you do it. You're not my man, but I thought you could be my guide.*

Bill brought her back to life somehow. He could bear her scars. He made love to them without judging, then he disappeared.

It was just past midnight, but it felt like years had passed since the rice cake with fresh basil cream cheese and the cheap CVS vodka.

When she woke up the morning after, she barely remembered what had happened. She fixed a cup of coffee and smoked a cigarette outside. The air was crisp—the sky gray and tired. She decided to go back to bed. She desperately missed his bodylines. Bill was her fix. And she needed to be in his arms.

Why did you come back? she asked. *For a book signing? I don't need you in public.*

I need your hands to touch me again, she wrote. *You are so handsomely hard against me, and I need your fingers, my tattoo bleeding. I need your hand on my neck. I need to feel the pain of when you pull my hair back with your sweaty hands. I want to be your slave, what did you do to me?* She put aside the notebook and took off her panties; she closed her eyes and almost sensed his bones from within.

It's your tongue, she whispered, *writing erotic poems on my skin. You want to hear me saying that; it turns you on when I beg for you inside me.*

K masturbated. It was the only alternative to cutting her wrist or hitting a vein or drinking thirty-five vodkas. She masturbated with the lights off, because she was too ashamed. And she did not want to give him the power of giving that pleasure to her. Under her silky sheets she lost herself in his memory, went to his caramel-colored leather couch, the breathtaking view from the terrace was beside her. K's hand became Bill's, so she started moving it inside her just the way he would in such a time of need.

Her heartbeat increased and blood seemed to be reaching the surface, raising her body temperature. Her hand was so violent that she didn't even feel human anymore; it was not hers. And, when her body faltered for the guilt of the self-induced pleasure, she finally surrendered to a private and silent orgasm. It was like having him there by her side.

K missed him, and not even her favorite cocktail made of Xanax and vodka could shut his presence out of her head.

The room was dark and untidy. Clothes had fallen off the bed and were now all over the floor. One of his old books was on the bed table, together with the two lavender candles warming and calming the empty, suffocating atmosphere lingering over the place, like a gypsy curse.

Bill was gone.

* * *

DAYS WERE PASSING BY. It was the end of July 1994. The book signing was scheduled to happen the upcoming week, so K had plenty of time to think about it, to consider all the pros and cons.

Her addictions were plentiful, but the one that ruined her was love. A dose of love, that was the only drug she both craved and ran away from. Love, a simple dose of pure, unbleached love, usually free, very addictive.

While thinking about Bill's book signing, K had managed to carry out some daily activities, wearing the professional mask during the day and keeping her habits hidden by night.

"I do want to see him again," K told Carrie when she got home after another boring interview for a TV show she had barely watched. "He's different, he is unlike any other man I've had."

"Then go," Carrie said. "Just be careful. You know he doesn't want anything serious, and you don't really know him."

"I feel like I've known him forever. There's something between us. I know he is kind of an asshole, but I don't want to have any regrets. I'm going sober, of course. No drugs. I can't take that shit anymore, Carrie. Not again, not if he's involved."

"Don't do it for him, K."

She grabbed a cigarette from the coffee table next to her and inhaled deeply. Carrie was right. Every time she had tried to quit in the past was to make somebody else happy or because they had caught her in her lies, whether it was her parents, a boyfriend, or a doctor who had to sign her dismissal papers. And it never worked.

"Maybe this is really just a book signing. We only had sex once, after all."

"Maybe. Do you want a tarot card reading?" Carrie asked, smiling to cheer her up with her psychic skills.

"Not tonight, Blondie, but thank you. I'm just going to have a drink, and think it over. You think I should go?"

"I think that when you find your soul mate you should never stop fighting for it. Whatever it takes."

"The Noose" by A Perfect Circle

The day had finally arrived. The only thing she needed that morning was a long walk by the ocean to clear her thoughts, to let the marine breeze wash away doubts and fears, the anger and the disappointment.

After walking barefoot for more than an hour with coffee in her hands, she sat facing the water. Recklessly touching her skin, while the sun was slowly rising above her head, she relished the salty iron smell that the ocean released into the morning air.

The pager she always carried around disturbed transcendence and brought her back to reality; it was almost ten in the morning and she had plenty of things to do before she made her decision about the book reading.

The first was a lunch meeting with her boss for a new project they had been assigned, together with a quick stop for groceries and coffee, since the apartment was completely empty. She loved shopping at Mrs. Gooch's when she could afford it. In a certain way, at least for what concerned her relationship with food, she was learning how to treat herself to something healthy when she was hungry after days of using.

After lunch, she decided that if she was actually going to go to Bill's book signing, she had to buy a new dress. The Chateau was quite elegant, and it would possibly be animated with some industry people. A new outfit was mandatory, and she would put it on her Italian credit card, with the endless list of debts she was accumulating.

K struck a deal with herself: she would think about the Bill issue after the meeting, which took place at the press agency's main office—a small apartment on Bronson Ave. It was an up-and-coming, hip neighborhood where young Hollywood liked to party, swinging between a French bistro and the many bohemian cafés where local writers would meet to brainstorm and feel less alone in the smoky darkness of their apartments.

Since the headache and the shaking wouldn't go away, she allowed herself some codeine: *Two pills,* she wrote. Not to get high, but because she couldn't handle withdrawal in such a circumstance.

After the meeting, she drove to Robertson Boulevard where, just a couple of days earlier, she had spotted a black cocktail dress that seemed to be the perfect choice for a twilight book signing.

She hadn't been in LA long, and kept forgetting how bad traffic was at rush hour; she was late and stuck on Santa Monica Boulevard, not exactly near the hotel. On the one hand, K was actually glad to be a little late, this way she wouldn't have the chance to meet him before the reading and if she changed her mind, she could leave without being noticed.

In twenty minutes of traffic, K had already smoked five cigarettes. *What the hell am I doing?* She asked herself while trying to find the perfect song on the radio. *Jesus Christ, I'm really doing this.*

Do you see yourself? Do you see yourself now? she asked herself. *Okay. You are making this choice, K. You are not high now, you had two fucking pills the whole day, and you are making this choice. You are very aware of what you are about to do, okay? No regrets tomorrow. Do you understand? No regrets!*

Once she got there she had one last smoke and stayed in the car for a while, just to prepare a mental escape plan.

Why am I here? she thought. *I don't even know if it's really for him. I don't know what the fuck I am doing*

here. I can't feel guilty for everything I do. Who cares if it's
a mistake? I'm allowed.

Guilt. While reading her journal, I couldn't help but
notice the recurrent use of that word. I kept wondering
why she was always feeling guilty for something. She was
always judging herself, her life, her actions and her plans—
nothing she did was ever good enough for her standards.

"K was special," Bill told me one day when I asked
him about her writing. "Her vulnerability on the page was
something so rare that I fell in love with the first story she
wrote. K would write what we'd all think and hide from.
She was brave."

"Did you ever tell her?" I recall asking.

"Many times, Angie," Bill reassured me. "I wanted her
to know that my obsession for her talent went way deeper
than our relationship. K was the real deal. She knew that
and it scared her to death."

Regret was the only feeling K never numbed. Regret
for letting herself go, regret for how she handled things in
Los Angeles, regret for not having planned in advance her
purpose in the city, just trusting Bill and his eye for the
alleged "true talent." Regret for spending money she didn't
have and weighing on her parents, lying to them about
everything she was doing with it. Regret for not feeling
appropriate and for not being able to fit in, regardless of
where she was. Regret for believing in stupid dreams, and
regret because she didn't know what she wanted.

"What kind of life am I living, Carrie?" She asked her
friend on a drunken night. "I feel like a zombie."

"What are you talking about?" Carrie asked, with her eyes and mind blurred by too much pot and not enough sleep. She was always interested in any kind of philosophical late night quest nonetheless.

"I'm supposed to be writing a damn novel. But I have all these questions in my head. It's all about these stupid numbers. Calories, money, debts. Half an hour to get from one place to another, thirty minutes, eighteen hundred fucking seconds stuck in traffic, listening to radio commercials when the Walkman's battery is dead, because I used it during the forty-five minute cardio session earlier, to burn the one hundred thirty calories of a non-fat yogurt and two rice cakes."

"Oh my God, Sweetheart. Breathe!" Carrie stopped her, worried about the amount of drugs in her body. "You're fucking high!"

"Hey, I'm not kidding, Carrie. I'm serious! And numbers are not the only issue. There's guilt. The too much or not enough shit! Why is there always something wrong? It's too much coffee or too many cigarettes, too much coke or too much Xanax, another pill, another fix. I'm getting more creative with my doctor every time. I don't have the energy to do that anymore. I can't remember a day without numbers.

"You know what's funny? I always hated math in school. I was never a numbers kind of girl. I have been a lot of girls, trust me, but definitely not a numbers one. So, how did I end up here?"

"Oh my God, K," Carrie said, amused. "Bill's right, you could write a book. Plenty of crazy in there," she said, pointing at K's head.

"You are just like me, Carrie. You smoke pot every day. But how many years must pass before we finally stop thinking about matching numbers? It's just another damn count; then it gets too late for a human brain to understand the equation for happiness. It's exhausting. I am exhausted. It all comes down to math, a scale of actions and a game where no one wins. It's just like in Vegas," she snapped her fingers. "No matter what, you lose."

No, math was definitely not her field of expertise. And, as in her life, in every relationship she always seemed to look for the wrong match, inevitably getting the wrong result.

Back in the car, in the parking lot of the Chateau Marmont, just time for a few drops of No. 5. K still wasn't used to the valet parking treat, especially if the event was a big one like this, but she kind of liked it. It made her feel important.

Even before entering the hall, she realized that she was not able to properly picture Bill's face or to reproduce the sound of his voice in her head. They had met only a few times before that evening. She tried to recreate the rhythm of his words, but the melody was disturbed. He was a stranger, and the only detail that awakened her memory was the touch of his skin, his smell, they way he moved his hands while talking, the way he moved them all over her body. But no voice came alive, and no clear visual images of his figure. She wondered if they really ever met, or if it had all only happened in her head.

In that moment, she just wanted to fly back home. She just wanted to be like all the people she knew: ordinary, apparently serene with their lives, able to enjoy small things, to live without pretending, without always looking for something more, something bigger, something stronger or whatever it was that she was reaching for, in order to find happiness outside of herself.

It was too late. Bill was already on the podium that had been set up for the event and he stared at her. He would never admit it, but he almost loved her, too, for the quicksilver frame of a lifetime that never was.

The Ultimate Road Trip

"Alice" by Tom Waits

K walked into the hotel and got carried away by the richness and elegance of the Hollywood glamour. The castle, the Chateau, is an iconic venue, an historical jewel on Sunset Boulevard. The hotel, built in 1927 and modeled after a French castle, is well known for its luxurious charm and for being a place of sin and buried secrets, so much so that its legendary guests never want to leave. Back in the golden age of Hollywood Vivien Leigh, Judy Garland, Greta Garbo, and Elizabeth Taylor, just to name some of those K had learned about, all spent time living at the Chateau Marmont. They all shared their darkest secrets in its mysterious and elegant rooms.

Bill, on the other side of the room, was already answering questions on his latest collection of political essays focused on the Cold War. K had two choices: she could listen to him, have a glass of champagne, and leave, or she could just wait for him to finish, be bold enough to congratulate him, and try to figure out what her real feelings were. She could use the old man as a mirror of truth. She was there and she needed to get to the core of what had happened between them.

Bill hid his discomfort on the stage like a professional actor. He didn't like book signings, and he did not particularly enjoy the act of reading his work in public, but he was good at it—sounding almost like a stand up comedian at times, with his famous gallows humor. K did not know him very well, but she could feel his thoughts, and sense his emotions. He liked independent bookstores better, but he felt honored and lucky enough to be alive and to be able to make a living out of writing.

When K realized that he had cultish followers there, she experienced a raging jealousy. Resentment boiled to the surface; they knew more about his works than she did. But Bill did not care about that, his eyes glowing thanks to her presence in the audience. In that moment she remembered what had brought her there in the first place. It was not the primal pleasure they shared that night, it was not the feeling of anger and revenge towards someone who had disappeared only to call her four months later, saying that he was sorry. She had real feelings for him.

He had awakened something within her, turned on a light that K never knew she had. The old man had brought something back to life. He was the reason why she was still in America, because he had seen honest talent in her. And she trusted him.

When the reading was over, she did not even care or worry about how she looked. He had the ability to make her feel beautiful, with him her permanently damaged anima was just an attractive and accepted part of who she was. Bill made her feel at peace and war at the same time, safe and in danger, sane and insane. Pain and painkiller in one drop, in one small, white pill. Bill Werber, poison and antidote, something highly and dangerously addictive.

> *I can feel it,*
> *I can feel your bones penetrating me,*
> *Your brain is nourishing mine.*
> *I feed on your hunger,*
> *I'll drink from your tears.*
> *You are going to die one day, I know*
> *But until then, we're going to live together.*
> *It might last a second or a month,*
> *But until you die, until we die, I am going to live*
> *with you.*

The audience was rapturous, K wrote on a page of diary as soon as she got home. She wanted to bleed the raw emotion of the night on paper. *They loved him. He has the amazing power of enchanting people the same way Japanese cherry black tea can enchant your senses on a cold afternoon. He has the romantic and melancholic touch that makes you shiver at the first look, at the very first note, at the very first spoken word of dark poetry. What Bill holds in his bones is the power of isolating body and mind in the middle of a loud crowd of a shopping mall in West Hollywood during Labor Day. I have always hated the holidays and their corny displays of colors or national flags. And he does, too. I have never met anyone like him.*

After signing copies of the book and thanking his audience, he got off the stage and headed towards K. She was talking business with a French journalist she had met months before, during a press junket in New York City, and did not quite acknowledge Bill's presence behind her.

When K and the man parted ways, Bill gently kissed her on the cheek, softly touching her long hair. She turned her face to him and their lips accidentally touched. What wasn't supposed to be a kiss at all became one of those movie moments, time stopped, a magical flow of energy took over. She had completely forgotten the touch of his lips, the way they tasted.

"Hey, stranger," she said, with her lips still close to his.

"Thank you for coming," he replied. The sweet tone of his voice disarmed K.

"Looks like an interesting read," K said, trying to make him understand how scared and nervous she was. "You knew I would…"

"No, I didn't. I'm no good at doing this, and I'm a big believer in feminine intuition. It wouldn't surprise me if I did not see you tonight."

Bill innocently touched the line of her upper lip, and kissed her again, deeper this time.

He has this way of engaging his tongue that is something deeper, more intimate than sex, K's diary from that night continues. *A rich entrée that fills me up. It didn't matter that we were in public, he licked my lips. And then entered them with such an elegant strength that the only thing I could do was surrender to it.*

"You are nervous," Bill said. "I can feel it. I'm sorry. I don't want to cause you any trouble. I just needed to see you again. I wanted you here, but I can't make any promise that I won't be able to keep." He paused. "See? That's the kind of ass I am."

"I didn't ask you to make any promise, did I?"

"No, you didn't," he admitted. "You never did, actually."

"So, I don't see a problem here."

"I needed you."

"Well, I'm here," K said, without looking at him, her eyes fixed on the floor.

They walked to the terrace and had a drink.

She ordered another glass of champagne and he stuck to tea. She didn't know what The Program was at the time. In Italy AA was not a big thing and sobriety was rarely an option. When you quit drugs, you could still drink beer—that's what Alex had done when he had gotten out of rehab. He drank and smoked pot; everything was allowed except heroin and cocaine. K barely realized she had a serious problem at this point. She stupidly thought Bill wasn't drinking because of a liver condition.

"Wasn't heroin your thing?" K asked pointing at the white cup he held in his hands.

"Yes, amongst the other things," Bill explained. "But you know how it works: alcohol was never a real issue," he continued sarcastic, "if I don't consider when I was an alcoholic."

"Do you mind if I drink?" she asked, as she needed a drink.

"Not at all," he said, drinking from his warm cup. "But you might want to try some tea one of these days. It's good for your health."

They shared a laugh that killed the tension for a second; K didn't want to argue about the past, but she had to ask him why he had disappeared after their night together. She didn't trust men, and she wanted an explanation for his behavior. K wanted to know why he took off like a twenty-five-year-old, leaving her with a lame note that read: *There's coffee beside your head, walking dog.*

After that night, they had kept in touch over the phone for a few days. He sent her the Frank Sinatra biography she had seen on one of the bookshelves at his place. But then, unexpectedly, he had disappeared. According to him, the reasons were many: it wasn't the right time, and he was old and sick. He described himself as a boring, solitary man with a schedule that was hard to clear. It was probably the truth on some level, together with the presence of a million women at his feet between his travels to New York and Europe. It wasn't enough to justify his actions, in K's eyes. She simply couldn't deal with a man not desiring her.

He owed her an explanation. Bill had the amazing ability to handle words and situations, and he always managed to do it in a gentlemanly way. Even when he was being mean or hiding behind poor excuses, he was able to make it sound at once right and poetic.

"I panicked," Bill said, without taking his eyes off her. "I am not used to waking up in bed with a woman next to me.

I wanted you to leave. I actually didn't even want you to sleep there, but it happened, as I didn't want you to drive at night." He didn't hide the embarrassment.

"When you left, I went to the meeting, like I told you. And when I came back I found your necklace by the bathroom sink. I freaked out, okay? I just realized you were not just a fuck and I didn't know what to do. I just don't know how to do this. I am not ready for a relationship and you left something in my fucking bathroom."

"I didn't leave it on purpose, Bill. I just forgot a necklace," K justified, well aware that the issue there wasn't the green necklace at all. "Is it because of what you told me when we were walking your dog?" She asked.

"What did I tell you?"

"That I am the whole package."

Bill smiled at her and tenderly touched her lips again, not hiding the desire for more.

"Well, you are quite a complicated one, K. But that's not the cause. We are two freaks, I guess. Every time I truly care about someone," he continued, "I just destroy it; I keep fucking things up. So I'd rather stay away. You are not in a position to be screwed right now. I'm not stupid, K. Maybe I'm wrong and it's none of my business, but I've been you."

At fifty-six, he was still figuring out how to handle life. How was he supposed to share anything, on any level, with a twenty-four year old? He had run away only realizing that he missed her when he found the green necklace. By simply holding it in his hands, Bill was bombarded with flashbacks of what they had.

When he sent the black letter, he did not think about the consequences. He did not consider what K's reaction would be; he knew he wanted her back. For a minute or for a lifetime, he did not know. At fifty-six, he behaved like a teenager that wanted his girl back and was determined to give it his all.

After listening to his words, K took a deep breath and hushed him with a long kiss. "Let's enjoy it without too much thinking, okay? I don't care for how long. Let's enjoy whatever this is right now," she said with disarming naïveté—a sensuality that at times made me hesitate, wondering whether it was rehearsed or if she truly believed in it. "And I want my necklace back. It was a gift."

After another passionate kiss, she told him about her busy day ahead, and that she needed to leave after one more kiss.

"By the way, this is my phone number," she said, smiling, while handing him her new business card.

"Thanks for coming; it was very kind of you."

"Goodnight, handsome, I really have to wake up tomorrow," she said, walking away and fearing a change of mind. "It was nice to see you."

They didn't talk the day after, but something unexpected happened the following Tuesday, in the middle of the night. K was still awake reading Bill's new autographed book, an essay on the seventies elections in Chile, in bed with a bottle of vodka. It was 3:00 a.m. and she couldn't sleep. She wandered toward the living room to smoke a cigarette and close the kitchen window, when she heard the phone ringing. She hurried to pick it up, as she didn't want to wake up Carrie. The ring was unexpected, and it scared her to death.

"Hello?" She whispered, managing the precarious balance of a tumbler in one hand, a cigarette in the other, and the phone tucked between her shoulder and her ear, with and too much vodka already in her body.

"Hey, it's Bill. I can't sleep."

"Neither can I," she said, sitting on the old brown leather couch.

"Listen, I had a crazy idea; I am going to San Francisco for four days, for work. I am leaving at six, tomorrow morning and I'm driving. I don't want to take another fucking plane. Wanna come along, by any chance?" He asked, just like he was inviting her over for a five o'clock tea.

"Bill, it's three in the morning. And I was in bed reading."

"What are you reading?"

"Your book," K admitted, embarrassed for not being able to lie and brag about a random title from her fairly furnished bookshelf. "The Chile Elections."

"And, you're not asleep? Wow, that's flattering. I gave you that book so you could kill roaches or hit your head to stop that talking inside of it, or your migraines. I didn't think you would actually read it."

"Oh, come on! You know I always read your stuff. And I love it, for what its worth."

"Well, that's very kind of you."

"Bill, it's late."

"I know, but do you remember when we had dinner in Santa Monica?"

"What about it?"

"I told you I would have to go up north for work, and I wanted to take you there."

"Oh, come on, you wanted to get laid that night, you would drive me to the moon on your broken Corvette to have me in your bed..." K laughed. She felt proud of herself for finally being realistic.

"Hey, I'm serious." Bill's tone of voice changed. "I'm not so predictable that I just need a fuck; I just want to take you to San Francisco, and I'd rather push you against a wall and ask you questions this time. I want to get to know you. Are you in?"

"Yeah," she hesitated. "I'm in, I guess."

"Bring warm clothes for a couple of days, okay? It gets cold up there!"

"You are crazy!" she said

"Ah! And what does that make you?"

K giggled.

"Don't be late. I have a dinner meeting, so we have to leave on time."

"I won't. But let me go now."

"Goodnight." And he hung up.

"Something in The Way" by Nirvana

K LOVED SURPRISES, ESPECIALLY from a man. But Bill made her nervous. It was three in the morning, she had seen him only a couple of days before after months of silence, and she had no clue why he had asked her along on a business trip.

She actually vaguely recalled talking about one of his projects up north during the dinner in Santa Monica, but she had truly thought he was just trying to seduce her with the idea of San Francisco. She never thought he was going to take her with him. Bill was apparently serious, or he had just become so a few minutes earlier.

She got up from the couch, finished her drink, and put the ashtray away. She fixed some coffee to wash away the vodka; for a second she considered the idea of a couple of lines from her well-furnished plate of cocaine. She moved the plate of cocaine aside, looking for clothes, and wondered if she could just flush it.

"I can't do it for him. I need to do it for myself," she whispered, with the dessert plate full of cocaine back in her hands and two bottles of codeine in the background, one partially hidden by a long black skirt. She touched the forget-me-nots decorating the rims of the plate and took a deep breath. "Not today, I would be doing this for him."

She swallowed two pills and took the two bottles for the trip; then put the plate aside again and chose a couple pairs of jeans, leather boots, and some sweatshirts. Her favorite blue-and-gray plaid shirt hung on the chair by the desk and she decided to wear it for the drive.

It was cold outside, being so early in the morning; she put a sweater on and added some special lingerie to her bag, together with a leather motorcycle jacket she had purchased in Camden Town, an original from 1985. She was ready for him. She poured a second round of coffee and smoked another cigarette. It was the only way to handle twenty-four hours without sleep. Peculiarly, against all her fears and with time ticking away, the anxiety started to fade away. She was not worried about Bill's proposal anymore. Everything seemed to be going exactly the way it was supposed to, adventurous road trip included.

Had everything been written before? Was there a plan or was it simply how life was supposed to show its inner and surprising beauty?

At 6:00 a.m. sharp Bill was downstairs waiting for her in the Corvette. The back window was still broken. For some reason, he had never found the time to fix it, and at one point K almost thought he kind of liked it that way. More to show off, to prove that he did not care about material things like expensive cars.

"I got coffee," he said pointing to a smoky paper cup when she opened the door. "Americano with just a hint of milk, right?"

"Yes," K smiled, quite surprised. "You remembered."

"My memory is slow," he said helping her to put the bag on the back seat, "but coffee I usually manage."

"Why didn't you fly?" K asked him, enjoying the liquid warmth penetrating her body.

"Because I've been living on a plane for almost four months now," Bill said, entering the freeway. "I couldn't take it anymore. I know you think it's glamorous, but it's exhausting after a while. Especially at my age."

"What's the meeting for?" K asked, unsuccessfully trying to hide her unstoppable hunger for details on Bill's life.

"A possible project I've been working on for a while," he explained, as usual not eager to talk about himself. "I wasn't even supposed to go this time, but they needed me on set for a day and I have this other meeting tonight, something I have postponed for quite a long time. So, I thought I would just drive. I needed to get out of Dodge for a while anyway. I can't stand LA these days."

"Thank you for asking me to go," K said. "It's been years since I last was in San Francisco."

"Are you kidding me? I have a young and charming Italian in my car. Who's the lucky one here?" And then he smiled. "This way you can drive when I'm tired; these meds are killing this old cripple you seem to like so much!"

Bill has such an amazing power of becoming the sweetest man alive when it comes to his health, K wrote. *It not only brings tears to my eyes, but he brings me onto my knees; he doesn't really seem to be suffering, but his vulnerability is lovable and tender.*

The ride from Los Angeles to San Francisco was about six hours long, quite exhausting, but so emotionally rich that it was worth every single mile.

K had the ability and sensibility to make a movie out of it in her mind. She didn't really care about how tired she would be at the end of the adventure, she was ready to be inspired by the beauty of the coast, by the power of her new lover.

"I have to be there for dinner," Bill said again while already on the road, "but I want you to see Big Sur, and maybe stop at the Henry Miller Library. Is it okay if we do that on the way back and drive the freeway now?"

"Of course," K said. "Do what you have to do. Business comes first."

"Maybe we can lay down somewhere," Bill added, slightly touching her leg. "To get some rest of course. Don't think I'm some kind pervert. You know, grab a bite." He looked at her for a second and then went back to the dead freeway. "Damn." He said, now taking his hand off her leg, almost like guilty for doing something wrong. "You are addictive, Jesus Christ."

K didn't say a word. She looked at him and attempted a seductive smile, bit her lips, and blushed.

She was well aware that nothing would change the anxiety and the fear. Bill made her feel agitated and calm at the same time. She feared him, to some extent, and maybe that power balance was the key that kept him there, by her side.

While driving and listening to Fleetwood Mac, they planned a couple of stops to get some rest and grab a quick bite. They were not after the elegance of some high-end restaurant. All they needed was food, something simple.

"Big Love" played.

This trip was exactly what K was looking for, just feeling the power of his wisdom, his past, Bill's experience, the road. Talking about their lives, their fears, and their truth—it wasn't just sex this time—there was a much deeper connection. He was the first American man she could speak of history and philosophy to, from Burroughs to Lenny Bruce, from Keith Richards to Charles Mingus, DeLillo to the Italian poet D'Annunzio—an author he didn't know and that she had introduced to him on their first date. She recalled him writing down the name on his black notebook, but she didn't think he would actually get his book of poetry from the library, *La Pioggia Nel Pineto (The Rain in The Pinewood)*. Bill's hunger for knowledge was fascinating. They learned from each other; the atmosphere they created made them want to stop at the first motel they found on the way.

They wanted each other, and the way he kissed her while driving took them to the breaking point. After a couple of miles, a motel sign showed up. Without saying a word, just looking into each other's eyes, they decided to add a stop to their schedule.

It was definitely the worst motel she had ever seen, in the middle of nowhere, not far from Fresno, right off the I-5 N. In a place that was possibly home to crackheads and deadbeat fathers kicked out of home in the middle of the night, Bill and K found a place to make love. The room was rundown and the lighting dark, but the grungy environment did not bother them. This time it was more than the first taste they had had of each other months before. It was about a deeper feeling, the truth, that left them vulnerable, pushed them past the point of no return.

We shared something more than similarities in our lives or a fucked up brain. We were more than two writers inspiring each other, K confessed, *and for as much as Bill would probably never admit it, we had just started to share our souls. For us, it was all about a word, a leer, a laugh; it was a tear when recalling death that never came, or an unwanted touch of hands. It was clear from the very first day we met. In that motel, we simply let go and became one.*

The spark that started it all was Bill's kiss, right in the middle of a discussion on his favorite quote from Voltaire's *Candide*—"Optimism is the madness of insisting that all is well when we are miserable."

Not a cheerful one, but cheerfulness rarely came out of his mouth. It was pure magic to K's ears. In a deep and intellectual way, he won K's heart back. They checked into the dirty motel because, like junkies, they needed their dose of each other.

There's a very thin line between sex and the need for feeling someone inside you, K explained, *and it was that something more that made the difference between us in Fresno.*

"I read a quote that made me think about you last night," Bill said while undressing her. "It's from Saint Augustine."

"What does the man say that made you think about me?" She asked whispering in his ear, breathing on his neck while unbuttoning his shirt.

"God, grant me chastity, not just yet." Bill continued with such a deep voice.

"I'll take that as a compliment," she said with her tongue on his lips, guiding him over her body. "I missed you inside me."

He gently opened her legs, laying her down on the bed. He adjusted the pillow under her head. She let him in, and they made love like the first time again. They restlessly loved each other, and when the dance was over, K looked him in the eyes and said, "I love you." She did not think about his reaction, didn't care about hearing it back from him. She just needed to let her feelings out, and when she did, she turned around and he put his arm on her hips.

"Don't say anything, please," she asked, ashamed. "It was just beautiful."

"It was," Bill said, kissing her shoulder.

What have I just done? She thought a few minutes later in the bathroom, while washing her face. *I LOVE YOU? What the hell was I thinking?* She looked in the tiny mirror above the sink and wiped a hole in the steam that clouded it. She moved closer to the wall cabinet and started talking to herself again. *Everything was going great, why did I have to ruin it with a fucking "I LOVE YOU?" Jeez!* She put some lotion on her face and stared at her reflection in the stained old mirror.

"Hey, you." Bill called from the bedroom, gently knocking on the door. "Is everything okay in there?"

"Yeah…" K said, paranoid he might think she was using again. "Give me one second and the bathroom is yours."

"Take your time," he reassured her. "I just wanted to make sure you were fine. I heard what you said in bed…"

"Hey," she stopped him. "I'm not in love, okay? I'll be right there." She took two more pills and walked out of the bathroom.

A long time had passed since she had said I love you to a man, and it had made the moment even more precious. It was probably not the most appropriate thing to do, but she felt dangerously alive. Her heart was clean.

They would have stayed in that nasty motel room forever, but traffic was unpredictable and Bill couldn't afford to be late for his dinner meeting. They had to get back on track and get to San Francisco as soon as possible. Just a smoke, a quick bite, and they were back in the car. She was driving this time; Bill wasn't feeling very well.

"Bad speed!" Bill humored as always. "That's what this treatment feels like, awful. Did you ever have bad speed?"

"Never did meth," K said.

"Sometimes I'd rather be dead than a cripple, barely able to make it out of bed. This treatment makes me feel strung out on bad speed. This shit gives you headaches that could crack walnuts."

"I'm really sorry, Bill," K said.

"No sympathy, please. I'm lucky enough I don't have to drag my ass to a fucking job. It is what it is, and I want to enjoy this with you. Just had to vent."

He was weak and tired and she had offered to drive. She liked driving anyway, even more with him by her side. She put on *Undertow,* a brand new album by Tool. Bill wasn't familiar with the band, but K remembered telling him about Maynard James Keenan, their singer, one of her favorites.

"Bill, trust me, you would love this guy. It's just up your alley, and he hates LA, too."

Bill laughed unusually loud. "I don't hate LA, it's just a company town for me. I go back and forth as to how I feel about the company."

"Wow, I've never heard you speaking so nicely about it."

"You know, in the past it's always been all about me. I was the 'fuck everything' kind of guy. I hated LA, I thought I was better, higher class."

"What changed then?"

"With time, I learned that in life it's almost never about us. And Los Angeles gave me a lot; I'm very grateful, believe me. I stopped being a self-centered asshole and life got a little better."

When Bill started to get it, digging deeper into Tool, she realized with joy and surprise that there was still something he could learn from a twenty-four-year-old writer.

It was about 4:00 p.m. when they arrived in San Francisco. Bill took a quick shower before heading to his dinner.

"I have to go," he said, kissing her. "Get some rest. I'll take you for a tour tomorrow, I promise."

"Go, I'm going to crash soon," She smiled, tired but happy. "You look handsome!"

"If I look handsome today," he said, "I really wonder who's the crazy one, between you and me."

"Go, you are late," K smiled and watched him walk away.

Without unpacking, she laid on the bed, put Nirvana on and closed her eyes, exhausted.

K knew that those days with Bill would not last forever. They were a detour from real life. She also knew that once back in Los Angeles, their real lives would be sitting in their living rooms, waiting for them—a temporarily untouched plate of cocaine and more codeine to be stolen, hidden in a closet, with a thousand unresolved issues that they both still had to figure out.

When Bill was back from his meeting, he was too tired to wake her up and talk. He was too tired to even take his clothes off. He took his medication and just let his body rest, with his leather jacket still on, next to K, his arm on her hips. And that's exactly how they woke up the morning after, and the two that came after that.

"They should make a bottle of you, baby," Bill told her the second morning after they had made love. He moved a lock of sweaty hair from her lips, "so I could take you with me with me everywhere. You should be illegal, too. I could get addicted to you."

"Don't," she hushed him with her finger, and then with her lips, terrified of what she had just heard, remembering the night up in the Alps, when she was just a girl, with Alex, no condom and the aluminum foil, the first vapor of heroin and what came thereafter. "Don't..."

"What?" Bill asked.

"The last time a man said that—" K explained, looking straight into his eye, "—was the first time I became illegal for real."

"Just become my little pill then, so I can take you everywhere," Bill smiled. "You make me feel good, and I don't remember the last time I said something like this to a woman in my bed, the morning after."

Twelve

"Love Hate Love" by Alice in Chains

Bill and K almost felt like a normal couple, shrouded by the fog and crisp wind of San Francisco. They knew that there was nothing ordinary about them as a couple, or as individuals for that matter. They both had issues to resolve. His health was in rapid decline, and even though K had tried to keep things under control, despite all her good purposes and intentions, she was falling into a downward spiral, physically and mentally.

She was losing control over her emotions and as a consequence, over food and drugs, as well. She needed drugs more than water. She was willing to lose everything for another thin line of pleasure and fast relief, for another pill, another glass, the last needle, or a new binge. It didn't matter who she had by her side; love worked its magic for a while, but in order to truly change, something had to radically evolve from within. Maybe somebody like K had to die or get close to it to appreciate life. Hiding a dessert plate in a closet for a weekend in the name of love was not enough.

"I've never reached the bottom." K explained to Dr. Carmen, when asked if she was tired of that nightmare, if she hadn't had enough of that torture.

"You reach the bottom when you surrender, K," Dr. Carmen said. "When are you going to surrender?"

"I can't," K confessed. "And even when I try, it doesn't last. Not even love is enough."

"Of course it isn't," Dr. Carmen said, considering that she was quite knowledgeable with K's coping mechanism by then. "Whatever you call love is just another drug for you; the way you use it. Do you know what codependency is? I'm afraid you are just substituting drugs."

The relationship she had with Bill was the living, breathing proof of it. She was okay for a week or two, but the spiral called louder than him. It had been going on for years and no matter where she was, no matter who she was living with, the voice was always there—screaming at times, whispering at others, never silent.

Her stomach could not handle the pain any longer. And that was the excuse for more and more pills. The wound on her left hand, caused by her teeth scraping on the skin when throwing up, started bleeding again; the old one had taken years to disappear.

Nose bleeds were a part of life, together with more frequent panic attacks that only a massive amount of

Xanax was able to keep under control. She started bingeing again once a week, a "treat" for being good and following her own stupid and deadly starving rules. And before she knew it the rule had become two days, then suddenly three, then almost every day, then more than once in the twenty-four hour days she had to endure.

I could almost see her, pure and empty, not beautiful, but swollen in her face. She would starve for four days and on the fifth, she would treat herself to a binge and purge night of punishment and purification. It was the day of rest according to her own personal bible.

"You look skinny. Are you throwing up again?" Bill asked her one night over dinner.

"You have no idea what goes on in my head. Let's not even start on this, please," she said. "You don't know what the voice tells you to do, how humiliating it is to listen to the insults in my head. You can't understand the cravings, Bill."

"I know bulimia, K," Bill said, facing her and sitting on the silver stool by the kitchen counter, waiting for dinner to be ready. "I know the pain and I know the lies, that's why I want you to talk to me, because I've been blind in the past. My sister was bulimic. So I probably can't understand the food thing, but hey, I've been a fucking junkie for twenty years, I think I can understand humiliation and shame."

"You can smell food, Bill," K said. "When you decide to eat it, you smell it from early in the morning and you know you are going to do it sooner or later, that's the only thing you will be thinking of, all day, until you finally throw up. It's just like getting loaded. The only difference is that you need a grocery store to score, a toilet, and a knife to cut yourself when you're done. At least, that's me. Do you really want to know how it feels after you eat?" She finally let herself go. "The shame? You feel so disgusted that you just want to kill yourself if you don't throw up. That's the truth. You feel so sick that you just want to die."

The first bite was the end. The first bite of forbidden fruit was the gateway for the beginning of the fall. There was no connection between brain and physical impulses; it was a primal instinct she was unable and unwilling to control, just like with a drink or with drugs. Nothing was ever enough.

Self-control is supposed to establish the difference between a child and an adult human being, based on social psychology textbooks. K had learned all the theories from the endless list of therapists that prescribed her pills and recipes to cure her mental state and she knew how the system worked. She lost the ability to dominate and balance her impulses and found herself a grown woman, out of control, just like a child—he wants the candy and he eats it.

Is there a way to make a U-turn and become a self-caring adult, or was she sentenced to life in prison?

K had tried to answer those questions for years. She was a prisoner in her own body and mind. The cage was more appealing than freedom. She couldn't blame anyone this time. She should have been able to overcome the past by now. Deep inside, she was already trying to find some sort of connection between the brand new fall and the brand new love.

Every day was getting harder and harder to handle. Bill traveled a lot for work and couldn't be as present as K probably wanted, needed, silently demanded. All their thoughts of enjoying each other without drama had faded away shortly after their honeymoon in San Francisco; they faded away just like a blow of smoke in a cold cloud of polluted air.

He had never lied to her. Since the very beginning, he had told her that he could not be in a serious relationship.

"You deserve more," Bill tried to make her understand. "You want the love story and you should go for it. Look at what I have to offer: What is this? Some kind of part-time romantic porn…"

Sex with him is a speedball, she wrote. *It's an orgasm just writing about it, and we both know it. But he does not let me in and it hurts.*

The relationship she shared with Bill was nothing like the one K had with Marco, with whom she could not remember any moments resembling reality. *We would have Chinese food at times,* K wrote, when trying to make peace with him in her mind, *always in a family-owned small restaurant around the block or we would eat spaghetti at home. We used to look at the city from far away, at dawn, like vampires ready to disappear, from the balcony of his tiny, reassuring, and smoky apartment. He lived on the seventh floor and the view was breathtaking. Our life, our love, was about getting high and drunk together, every night, same place, same time.*

I talked to Marco, although he was very reluctant at first and English wasn't his native language. But I believe he cared for K and made an effort. All I can say is that they were both very sick. He was out of control as much as she was, challenging life and venerating death more than actually enjoying each other. It was fun for a while, at the very beginning, until they both started getting loaded after coffee, Marco with beer or whisky, K with cocaine and her empty stomach. One day, they were not able to stand each other sober anymore. K was getting high every day, first thing in the morning, until the thought of that final cardiac arrest or the overdose had become her primary goal.

They walked dirty roads of life together before the violent fights came. She got lost, some kind of ghost. K had become the shadow of her own lies, nothing more than a breathing disappointment to her own eyes. She needed Marco's presence and did not even care about how damaged they were together. It was clear that he did not love her. That is why she could not wait to get loaded and be somebody else with him, to have the fake partner she wanted him to be, the one that for a couple of hours seemed to be committed and willing to protect her.

They would not talk for hours if they didn't have alcohol or drugs in their blood. Not a good morning when waking up, not a kiss, no hands touching, just the worst coffee in town, cheap Chinese food, and a T-bone steak, once in a while.

She did not know what was wrong with her. But she just could not leave, not even when he asked for his apartment keys back. She could not give up on him.

He became food, blood, and dope to K. And she was his drink to escape a world he hated. Not willing to surrender to the obvious, opening her eyes to a reality she didn't want to accept, K always came back, forcing her way into something that just wasn't meant to survive. Marco always promised everything would change, perhaps genuinely meaning it for a minute or two.

So together they remained. But on a winter night he made a mistake she wouldn't be willing to forgive.

Like any other night, they had drinks at one of their favorite clubs, just a couple of miles north of Turin, where music played loud, shades were dark, and liquor flowed freely. K wore thigh-high boots and a denim miniskirt, blood red lip-gloss, and thin black eyeliner. She remembered Marco's clothes, too; vintage blue jeans and an old navy T-shirt with holes in it.

The place was dark and smoky. The walls painted dark red and the floor a hypnotic pattern of checkerboard black and white squares, sticky with alcohol and cigarette butts. Lights were low and warm, and the eighties music created the perfect atmosphere for a night made of sins and final decisions. The place had become a familiar spot for them, usually arriving at around four in the morning, when most people were ready to leave.

While he was drinking at the counter, she was doing cocaine with friends in the kitchen. Maybe it was the music, maybe it was the adrenaline, or maybe she was pushing to get the attention of the man she loved, but that night seemed more extreme than usual.

Everything seemed ordinary when she decided to grab a drink from the main counter in the other room. From the kitchen in the back where she was partying, she walked to the main dance floor and almost collapsed from shock; it was too much for her to handle. Marco was on the small couch by the entrance, his hands on her breast, and his tongue on her—a tiny brunette she had never seen before. K's lover was completely drunk, and cheating on her without even hiding it, proudly showing off in front of her eyes. She was familiar with his past cheating history; women and whisky were his things and he hadn't changed for K.

Completely drunk and on the bad side of a high, K did not know what to do. She couldn't face him. K just wanted him out of there in that exact moment. In screaming tears she asked her friends to do something and Marco left with the girl.

The day after, she was so ashamed and devastated that she decided that the relationship with him was finally over, he would be the last man she let into her heart.

K couldn't even get out of bed. Hours slowly shuffled, and she couldn't move, completely paralyzed. She was a ghost, emptied, hopeless and with no direction.

"Now you understand why I do this?" She told Dr. Carmen.

"Honestly, K, I do not," Dr. Carmen said, surrendering her hand on the desk that separated her from her patient, not even looking at her. "Help me understand, please. I know you hurt, but hurting yourself even more doesn't help."

"Can't you see it?" K asked the doctor, as if she was blind or stupid. "Can't you see what happens every time I try?"

"You were not trying, K." Dr. Carmen finally came down on her more like a mother than a therapist, referring to what had happened with Marco, someone that Dr. Carmen had never liked. "Stop lying to yourself. How were you trying this time? By getting high, but doing it with him? He hurt you, so you decided that it was better to go back to cutting your wrist and keep throwing up? Is that what you're saying? That this is the kind of pain you can handle better by yourself? A bottle of Xanax and you go back to doing heroin so the pain goes away in your bed?"

She understood that fooling the doctor wouldn't be so easy anymore, that Xanax prescriptions from her were out of question from that moment on. "You know what? It's pointless, you don't understand. The hour is over now. I'll see you next week," K said, grabbing her purse and walking away.

Days dragged themselves by, and Marco never called. Neither did she.

I know I am not the chosen one, but if you are listening, she cried in the darkness of a bedroom that had become her prison. *If you are there, I beg you, let me go.*

Kill me now, for I cannot walk.

Kill me now, for I cannot move. I'm slowly vanishing.

Mow me down and let me be your first. Or bless my life again, because I cannot do this alone.

I look at my face in the mirror. And I'm nothing more than junk.

You know, God, how does it feel to be chained and paralyzed? I am scared; they're watching me and I can't see a light from here.

Have you ever crossed the threshold? They say you were human in another life; you know how that feels. You know the pain, but there isn't even hurt or grief. That's why I need the blade, some kind of warmth.

Are you laughing up there? How many times have you been asked for a miracle like this?

I can pay you off, little by little. Or, I can be your slave in heaven, if you will demand it so.

I know the nature of my actions perfectly classifies me for purgatory, I'm the perfect candidate, but mercy is all I'm asking for.

She fell asleep with bleeding eyes that night. K thought she had reached the bottom.

You are Better Off This Way

"These Days" by Nico

Her relationship with Bill was different than the love she was used to, and still managed to function in a way she seemed to be unable to escape. That deep understanding and loyal inspiration binding them together was not enough, at least not for him.

He had become more than a lover for K. Bill had become a mentor, someone who could truly understand K's war and search for serenity.

She couldn't resist his hands on her skin, there wasn't a part of Bill she could resist. He was getting older but the daily gym routine and his gourmet vegetarian diet seemed to cover up all those years of heroin and self-loathing. His arms and his back were beautifully designed, not too much, just the perfect blend of flesh and texture, age and remembrance of youth. She loved his tattoos, even if she didn't know the meaning of them all, and even if his very own memories for some of them where blurred after so many years.

"I woke up with this one years ago," he told her one night pointing at a black bird inked on his inner arm, the right one. "It's like having sex with a stranger and waking up with her without memories. The only difference is that you have to live with a tattoo for the rest of your life."

After the last poisonous feminine presence Bill had had by his side, the last thing he wanted and needed was to get into any kind of trouble again with a woman. K was the shadow of more trouble.

Maybe he was not ready. Maybe it was a lie. Or, maybe he was just done with it all. He never got married for love and intimacy was still a pill he could not swallow without pain and worry. No matter how hard K had tried to prove to him that she was different, there was nothing she could do to break the chains of his heart. And, if the other option was having a life without him, she was more than willing to accept the compromise of the non-relationship.

Dark moments of silence were common for an artist like him. There were times when she missed him, especially during his frequent, long stays in New York, but she was aware of what she had gotten herself into when she had decided Bill was the one—complaints were not included in the package.

After their trip to San Francisco, back in Los Angeles, K began using again, more and more every day, without admitting to herself that she was losing the ability to say no. She was slowly returning to hell, increasing her already severe debt with an Italian bank and stealing more money from her parents.

When it came to Bill, however, she was very careful and tried to not use as much around him. He seemed not to have noticed how bad the situation was becoming again. They were not seeing each other very often anyway. She knew how to hide it, and at the first stages of relapse, it was easy to do so without being caught.

"It will all turn around," he had said. But everything seemed to be turning back.

In fact, things at Bill's were about to go south. And the best excuse he could find to escape the constraints of a romance, an almost-love he could not bear, was reversing all his rage on K. Self-pity and fatigue had taken over him, together with his frustration over a career that had not taken the right turn after the publication of his book. His documentary never made it into Sundance; and it was heartbreaking. His manager dropped him at last.

They were having dinner a couple of days after he had returned from a trip to New York. Conversation ran fluently over a home cooked meal of eggplant parmigiana and apple tarte tatin. Dodger stadium was lit up and the terrace looked more beautiful than it ever did before. He had bought two new wooden chairs. Lila sat against the wall, near the glass door. The ashtray was empty and still on the little dusty coffee table between the two new chairs. She had not smoked since she had arrived there.

K was momentarily happy. She didn't care if he was older and would never be able to give her any kind of stability, or a child, for that matter. Bill was the one, and she was ready to accept the consequences of her choice. The dream of giving birth to a child had been a selfish one. Every time she thought of having kids it was to reassure her soul, to leave a part of her in this world, or sometimes just a hopeful feeling that she wouldn't end up old, wrinkled, with aching bones, alone in her private shelter with only a view on the world she had deliberately escaped from.

"You might want to have a ring here, someday," Bill told her, kissing her hand. "I won't be able to do that for you, K, you know that."

"Bill," K said, becoming very serious and taking away her hand. She would have wanted his lips on it forever, instead of a gold band. "You should know me by now; I don't have to have a diamond ring on my finger while shopping for expensive baby clothing in Beverly Hills to be a woman." She felt powerful in that moment, so powerful that she stood up and continued her speech in a presidential way, proud of her words, even if she just wanted him to hold her tight.

"I don't want to become one of those frustrated housewives, hiding behind Botox while wondering how old the new assistant that's screwing their husband is. That is not really my plan. I just want to write, and if there's a partner by my side, well, that's cool. But I know how it works; I see those women." She sat down and slowly moved her hand close to Bill's lips.

He smiled at her.

"Why this question again?" She asked.

"Because at this stage of my life," he explained, "I am at a point where I don't want to hurt anyone. And you are too young to make these kinds of choices."

She knew he had been feeling worse lately, and she also knew that he wasn't in the mood for dinner, a date she had forced on that occasion. He was tired and felt uncomfortable because of his unkempt house.

She hadn't noticed any mess in the living room, things were pretty much where they were supposed to be: a couple of books on the couch, a calculator on the coffee table, and maybe a scarf hanging from a chair. But she loved the random order of things in there.

The kitchenette was a dirty and non-functional little spot in the middle of the easy and cultured luxury of the place.

It looked like he had not used that section of the house in over a decade. She pictured him on a regular day at home by himself, ordering dinner and eating in front of the TV, watching a documentary on the war in Bosnia. Any detail of his life would fascinate her, and small daily habits were her obsession, like watching through a window and thinking of stories about the characters in it.

K always loved observing people, since she was a kid. *I remember staring at their window,* she wrote in a page of her Los Angeles diary. *It was usually at dinnertime, after dusk, when the father had come home from work. The warm light from their window always appeared to be more reassuring than mine somehow. For I always felt something was missing. I would just stare and dream about what they would do at home; I would feel their love by osmosis, feed on their warmth from far away, with elegant Venetians separating our breaths. Years later, I realized that my obsession for watching and being watched was also touching my sex life, but that's not the point,* she continued.

She explained her theory almost like she knew someone would read her words one day. *It was their rhythm and their gestures, their habits and rituals. It was like watching a black and white movie, or living my own life through theirs; something like denying my very own feeling alive to embrace someone else's. I have never understood why, until I realized that I was enjoying other people's lives more than mine. My obsession had turned into envy.*

That is probably when I decided to welcome disorder into the picture. For it made my life more similar to the one I imitated, from time to time; or so I thought, in my arrogant and victimized, fearful mind.

There was always jazz playing happiness through their window. There was wine and laughter, there was some kind of beauty. Everything looked perfect, like out of an elegant page of Elle Décor, *with the latest trends on the interior design scene. Lights were always brighter than those shining in my family's apartment. My living room always seemed cold and colorless, very close to a silent film.*

Most of the time in those dreams, it was cold outside, New York or Chicago, a mountain cabin, or a beach house. Winter was my favorite season to observe and paint in my head, for I believe I have always been a masochist somehow.

What hurt me the most were the contrasts in temperature, the cold outside and the fire inside. I remember hot chocolate, too, and Earl Grey. My characters always drank something hot and wore wool sweaters to keep warm. I like the itchy feel of wool on my skin.

Over the years, this obsession made her feel isolated and different from her peers, so lonely and unhappy that it became the only way she could engage with the world.

Back at Bill's, at around 10:00 p.m., he suddenly stopped kissing K and pushed her away.

"What's wrong?" K asked. "You ok?"

"Listen…"

"Wow, that's some serious voice, did I do something wrong? I thought we were having fun."

"We are having fun, K, and I loved dinner, it was so awfully kind of you to cook for me, I'm not used to it, trust me. And you are beautiful tonight."

"So, what's the problem?"

"You can't sleep here tonight."

"Are you serious? Bill, listen, you should know by now, I'm not one of your whores you call in the middle of the night from your hotel room. I fucking love you. I'm so stupid that I care for you."

Bill had never seen that kind of rage and disappointment on K's face.

"I never thought you were my whore, K; I never treated you like one, I never deliberately wanted to harm you in any way, it's just that…"

"It's just what?" K screamed, waiting for his answer.

"I'm sick, for Christ's sake! Don't you fucking get it? It's not always about you or us. I crash like an old fart and I sweat. I wake up puking. Do you have any fucking idea of how that feels? I told you, this is what happens when you don't die young. So you better hurry up if you don't want to end up like me. I haven't said anything so far because it's none of my business, but I'm not blind. What are you on tonight?"

Bill grabbed her hand, when she attempted to walk away.

"Don't be stupid. Where are you going?"

"Let me go," K said, not convinced of her own words. She hated herself for what she was about to do, but she surrendered and pushed her body against his.

"I want to be with you, Bill. I don't care what you look like at three a.m. I want to be by your side, is that so hard to understand? I want to help you."

"K, listen, I'm not your kind of guy, okay?"

"Bullshit! What about San Francisco?"

"That was a moment, K. I thought a lot about it, and I just can't do this right now."

"Be a man. You are just full of shit. You keep living in denial, in this beautiful cage you've built for yourself. Will you ever realize that you can have something else, and that not every woman that falls for you is a slut after your money or a psycho?"

I couldn't believe she wrote almost the entire conversation. I don't know if it was for her book or to remind herself of the pain she felt in that moment, that she wasn't willing to experience anymore, but she just wished she had her weapons with her. She needed a drink, or anything that could make the discomfort disappear, his rejection impalpable. The equal opportunity junkie was back. The nature of her fix was not important, as long as it delivered and washed life away.

She reached for her purse and put her coat on. She didn't even look him in the eyes.

"K, wait," he said.

"What do you want from me?"

"Just don't leave like this."

"You are the one pushing me away, Bill."

He violently grabbed her while she was already on the stairs, almost to the door.

"Take this off," he said almost whispering with his rough voice, tugging at her coat.

He undressed her without even listening to what she was saying. She started crying and then kissed him.

"Please, Bill. You will never give me what I want. I was stupid to think you could."

She remained naked, and he was completely dressed. He pressed her body against his, almost like to protect her naked vulnerability. He gently caressed her hair and kissed her shoulders.

"I want you, but I can't have you here in my bed. You won't see me like that."

His hand was already inside her. K was wet and he moved deeper and deeper, before she dropped to her knees and unzipped his jeans.

Bill stopped her and took her hand. He got onto his knees and took her face in his hands.

"You are not like the other women, K. But I have to let you go. You deserve more. I care about you."

She moved her face and kissed him.

"Let me stay here tonight, then I'll disappear." she whispered in his ear.

They made love where love was about to end, on the gray carpeted stairs, and his naked body never looked so beautiful, dangerous, and wrong.

When it was over, Bill went into the kitchen to get some water. When he got back to the stairs, K was gone.

What Happens in Vegas...

"Confusion" by Alice in Chains

After that night, Bill decided that it was better and safer to stick to whatever kind of long distance, professional correspondence they could afford. K didn't agree with it, but he seemed to be getting everything he wanted from her. He had made a decision and there wasn't much that she could do to change his mind.

She would miss his dirty kitchen with the broken sink, and his leather couch with Lila sleeping on it. Every time she had driven up there, the lights of Los Angeles from far away had filled her with some kind of superhuman energy. When K was his, nothing really mattered, just the time they shared.

Bill's health was getting worse and K's would, too, if she didn't put some distance between the two of them. For as much as she hated being away from him, she had to acknowledge that what Bill had decided was for the best.

K's brother was visiting Los Angeles from Italy the week after the tumultuous sex on the stairs incident and she was really excited they were about to spend some time together. She had not seen her brother in months.

"Sweetheart," Carrie told her the afternoon before K's brother arrived. "Try to enjoy the time with him. You will deal with Bill, just not now."

"I wanted to be sober for my brother, Carrie," K said. "Jesus, I'm a fucking mess. I seriously need to stop, or it will get out of control again."

K had hated Alessio for so many years that she wanted the Los Angeles vacation to be perfect for the two of them, a beautiful memory that he could bring back to Italy as a souvenir. He had always been considered the "good one" in the family, and his humble, quiet perfection had always made K look even more wrong and out of control.

Nevertheless, when she had moved far away, they had started exploring the sibling bond. His visit was happening at the right time, or so she thought. Because not even the presence of a close family eye on her prevented her from giving in, and sinking deeper into the drugs, getting closer and closer to her last bottom. Relief was the feeling she was after, but guilt and shame soon took over. She was about to betray one of the few people who had the same level of deep sensitivity and who had never stopped loving her, even in his inexplicable silence.

The first week in Los Angeles with Alessio was beautiful. K managed to hide her secrets pretty well in between a visit to the Hollywood sign, Griffith Park, and a gusty drive to Malibu.

"You look tired, Sis," Alessio told her, completely unaware of the fact that her nose bleed on the way back from Santa Monica wasn't really from low blood pressure, but a nauseating amount of cocaine. "Let me drive. You have been working all night and you are driving me around every day. You need to stop or you will crash again."

"Don't worry, bro," she reassured him. "I'm okay. Don't I look better already?"

They were finally spending some intimate time together, and K didn't want him to find out she was the same sister he remembered.

"I'm really happy you are here, Ale," she said, looking into his eyes. "I mean it."

K, Alessio, and Carrie spent the following weekend in Las Vegas. Being Alessio's first time, their plan was gambling in every casino in town, while enjoying the insanity and the noise of the Strip.

"I feel it," K laughed, excited, but already high, after a couple of stops in some freeway restrooms.

"You feel what?" Alessio asked, still in the car, in the hotel parking lot, before the check-in.

"This weekend is the one. I am going to pay off all my debts," she laughed. "I am going to pay Mom and Dad back this time, for real."

"You are kidding, right?" Alessio said, almost like he was the older brother. "Because if you are serious you will end up very disappointed, and you are going to ruin all the fun."

"C'mon!" K argued. "Could you dream big for once in your life for Christ's sake?"

"K, grow up," Alessio said, annoyed. "Can you have fun like a normal person for once?"

The trio started at the Mirage, after which they walked through the old-fashioned charm of the Sands, the same floors Sinatra and Judy Garland had touched, where shady memories and eternal legends were the house special.

Unfortunately, at the end of 1994, the casino was just a shadow of the place it used to be. But it still was a landmark, and she didn't want to miss it.

Although the glamorous flashback of the Golden Age captured her attention, her mind could not sit still. She took a photo with her brother and couldn't stop shaking. The occasion deserved something more than just cocaine, which she had left in her room to be a normal person for at least a couple of hours, but she just couldn't handle it. She took a couple of pills, but it wasn't enough. The craving was preventing her from being at least decent in front of a brother she had not seen in months. So she grabbed another drink and started thinking about an excuse to leave. She actually had not checked her voice mail for two days, and decided she would take a break from the gambling to just go back to her room, alone.

K stopped to look at her face reflected in the mirror of a souvenir shop, in between a cheap shot glass and a miniature of a slot machine. She was exhausted. She had lost a lot of weight, and even though her eyes held some kind of a charm, a hint of color, they had lost every trace of life. She could barely breathe through her nose. She tried to chew one of those sugary pink bubblegums that made her feel cool at the very beginning of her cocaine love, but it did not work. Nothing worked any more.

K, Alessio, and Carrie all walked out and went for a bite at the Peppermill. The restaurant was a legendary symbol of the strip, with its exotic and dim atmosphere of vapor and fire.

"Let's sit there!" Alessio screamed, excited as he saw the fire and the steam coming out of the indoor pool.

K wasn't hungry, but some warm food would help her feel better, since the drugs didn't seem to be working.

When their dinner arrived, she barely touched the tomato soup she had ordered, but ate a cracker, and left twenty dollars on the table, while Alessio and Carrie enjoyed their burgers and fries with chocolate milkshakes.

"You should eat something, Sis. You look pale," Alessio said, slightly touching her arm with a beautiful innocence, completely unaware of what was really going on in his sister's head. "C'mon, we are here to have fun and you are not. Don't tell me it's because you are not winning?"

"No, Ale," she attempted a smile, loving her brother in that moment as she had never loved him before, for being so pure and so beautifully untouched by her struggle. "It's not because I'm not winning. Just too many people, you know me… I'm just a bit tired, I guess I need a cup of coffee."

"Are you okay?" Alessio asked. "You don't really look good."

"I need a walk," she said, shaking and visibly upset. "I'll meet you back at the hotel."

She smiled, touching his hair to reassure him. "I'm okay, I promise. I just need a walk and I am going to check my voice mail back at the hotel. Haven't checked it in two days and the office might have called. I was on a deadline. Don't worry. I'm fine."

"K," Carrie grabbed her arm before she could walk away.

"What?" K said, elegantly annoyed by all the delay they were causing.

"Don't call him," Carrie whispered, trying to keep Alessio out of it, since she didn't know if K told him about Bill. "Your brother is here, don't screw up this weekend."

"I am not calling fucking Bill!" K said loudly. "I'm taking a walk, and checking my voice mail." She gathered her hair into a careless chignon, pretending she wasn't affected by the sound of his name. "I'll meet you back at the hotel and we'll go back to making some big money, okay?"

She walked to the hotel and smoked a cigarette. Finally alone, K headed to bathroom cabinet.

I quickly pulled out the bag from my beauty case. I emptied it on the bathroom counter and pulled out the cocaine straw from my wallet. I snorted the first very thin line like a starving kid would eat a piece of bread.

She thought she could face the world like that; she thought she could face her messages. There was nothing work-related waiting for her, but a new voice mail from a woman she didn't know.

Her name was Vera, and she was a woman from Bill's past that had tracked K down through an interview she had read with her name on it. The very first one from when K moved to Los Angeles, the day she met Bill.

She listened to the voice mail twice. In between a compliment—*I'm a big fan of your writing*—and a cliché—*I wanted to hate you but I love your words so much that I can't*—Vera floated into K's life.

Jeez, K thought, exceptionally clear-headed, given the high she was on, *who the hell is she?* "I need to talk to Carrie," she said to herself.

She got up, washed her face, and put some lipstick on. She was sweating and felt nauseated all of a sudden.

I look awful, she thought, considering the idea of still playing the drunk card with Alessio. *Wait,* she smiled at herself in the mirror. *I am not that bad after all, I am just judging myself too much. I could be dead, and I'm here, feeling pretty awesome apart from this freaking nausea.* "Ginger ale!" She said out loud, lighting a cigarette and cleaning up the white powder residue on the bathroom counter with her finger, and licking it up.

They were supposed to meet in half an hour, just the right time to become presentable again. It took her some effort, but she still seemed to look somewhat normal.

That is probably why, for a long time, most of her friends never really saw what she was doing to her body, how she was hiding drugs. The surface of her body still blessed her with some kind of glow, that is why she always got away with it.

Vera knew exactly which cards to play with K. When you are obsessed with someone, everything takes you back to the obsession. Every detail becomes a photo of your own story, or the smell of a bedroom where sex was wild and passionate, where memories are sweet.

That's the first impression K had about Vera. She dismissed and underestimated the woman as someone who could not get past an old love story, nothing more and nothing less. But was she really entitled to any judgment? How well did she really know Bill?

"Anyway," the voice mail ended, "you seem a real doll, so just be careful with Bill; he is not who you think he is. Call me if you want to talk. Ciao."

K meditated on whether the woman was telling the truth, if Bill could be the cause of all the pain and the trouble, infecting people with the contagious virus of misery.

K had never met the woman, hadn't even heard of her. Or maybe she had without knowing, since Bill never gave names away, so secretive about the details of his personal life that hadn't been made public by the media through the years. K was well aware of Bill's past, especially of his history with women, but getting such an intimate confession from a stranger was upsetting.

Bill and K had not been talking since the fight at his place. He had disappeared, and made no contact with her. She was miserable, but no matter how much she hated him in that moment, she felt she had to ask him for advice.

Alessio and Carrie would arrive shortly, and she didn't have much time left. K walked outside, on the terrace, feeling somehow cool for being the drama queen of the night. Through Vera's phone call, she felt privileged by still having a connection with Bill.

Like always when it was about him, K wrote in the diary full of rage and resentment, *Bill left me a voice mail right away—stilted words. Baffling how such a talented writer could articulate so poorly when it came to real life.*

"Be careful of Vera. Do not respond with more than a cursory reply. I'm serious, K."

She ignored the sterile warning and, once back in Los Angeles, called the woman back. After politely thanking her for the compliments on her writing, K also made it very clear that she did not know Bill other than for that interview, months before. She wanted to be cautious, but her first thought was that, after asking for advice, the least Bill could do in that situation was stand by her side, at least explain who Vera really was.

She hoped for a sign of support and protection from him. He gave her indifference. Like she was a stranger, like San Francisco never happened.

That Afternoon in Paris

"Sympathy for the Devil" by The Rolling Stones

K, Alessio, and Carrie were back in Los Angeles the day after Vera's voice mail. K's mind couldn't be anywhere else but on Vera's follow up phone calls, now at K's office. K never replied to Bill's warning. She did acknowledge the danger, but she was so angry for the way he had treated her that she made the conscious choice to stop trusting him.

She decided to be smart and not reveal personal details to Vera. The woman was able to win her over so quickly that it almost felt like Bill's absence was being replaced by the haunting presence of his former lover.

K never wanted to hurt him in any way. She loved him, but she naively thought that, since he had left her for no reason but fear of giving their non-relationship a try, she could indulge in a leftover piece of him. K thought Vera was the woman Bill had loved the most, or at least that's the perception she had from what the woman was conveying. She had been the one in his life, and no one else could ever replace her in Bill's heart.

"Leave it alone, sweetheart," Carrie warned her. "This is turning into too much drama." Even Carrie suggested she turn the page and forget about him. K did sense the danger at that point, but seemed more inclined to challenge it, than to avoid it. She poured herself a drink and sat next to her friend on the couch.

"Maybe I can find some closure by talking to her," K said. She had lost that last bit of Vegas street allure. Her condition would soon become visible to everyone. Neighbors could smell the cocaine smoked on the stairs and everybody could see her difficulty breathing. Her nose bled, constantly. "It hurts, Carrie; I don't know what to do."

"You are not seeing things clearly," Carrie said. "He told you to be careful, you are not listening to him. And, you are high."

"What does that have to do with anything?" K asked. She was annoyed by where the conversation was headed. "I am just trying to talk," she screamed. I don't know if it was the Italian blood or just too many drugs combined together at that point, but her emotions were out of control. "Why does it always have to come down to what I do?"

"Sis," Alessio interrupted, softly, almost afraid of stepping into something he wasn't allowed into. "Carrie is right. You are not okay. I am leaving LA tomorrow, K. I want to know you will be fine."

They were worried for her, but in that moment they couldn't understand that Vera's words had hit K hard. Scared and angry as she was, she'd rather trust the stranger.

The night after Alessio went back to Italy, while reading on the couch, K warmed up with a glass of cheap red wine from the closest liquor store around the block. All her money was being spent on drugs lately, and if she had to choose between good drugs or good alcohol, the first option was the healthiest one—a bad dose could kill and she was still bargaining with life. *I want to die*, she wrote. *But there's something still holding me here. I wish I could make up my mind.* A three-dollar bottle of red was good enough with some codeine.

She closed the book and her eyes. Nirvana played and the cocktail of Xanax and codeine finally began to melt her blood; it allowed her breathing to become smooth. K relaxed, and wished she could be Vera for a second. She was well aware that she could be making a huge mistake by letting the woman in. She also knew that she couldn't trust her and that Vera knew better, she could smell Bill on K's skin. Vera was just waiting for the right moment to attack and shoot the final bullet. Any information she could get would be used against him.

Still on the couch, completely dressed and too high to take off her clothes, she wondered why Bill wasn't even asking her how she was, and how she was holding up with Vera's alleged danger.

She checked her pager again and saw no sign of him, though his ex was sneakily slipping into her life and back into his.

"Why do I have to love him?" she cried.

It was on that night, too tired to think straight, when she decided to meet Vera. She got up to get some water and a cigarette and called her to take her up on her coffee offer for the day after.

The weather was about to change, and there was an unexpected downpour, she dressed her best to meet the enemy at the small French bistro she managed.

She woke up at 6:00 a.m. nervous for the "friendly" coffee ahead. Her hands were shaking from an early morning withdrawal. She really needed a fix, or maybe she knew she was making a huge mistake by meeting Vera. But she reached for the almost-empty bag of cocaine on her bed table. She prepared two thick lines to wake up, with what little melted ice and vodka left was next to the black lamp, still on from the night before.

The meeting was scheduled at 5:00 p.m. and by that time she would be so high she wouldn't even care about the consequences. She couldn't flake, K was intimidated by Vera and missing an already scheduled coffee date could piss off the woman, and she didn't want that.

"It's just one time," K said, while trying to hide the scars on her arms with some ivory powder and a slightly darker foundation, sitting on the bathroom floor, in her lace panties, ready to get dressed. "One time," she repeated, making sure to pronounce clearly every letter of those two words, o-n-e t-i-m-e, while the white paste covered the cemetery of thick wounds, like oil on canvas.

She wanted to see what Vera looked like.

"She can't be beautiful," she said to herself when the scars were partially covered, and moved to fix her eyes, to make them look like those of a healthy young woman.

I want to hear what her voice sounds like, she thought then. *Just for five minutes, I need to see what I'm not.*

K had lost Bill, and if he had really loved Vera so much, she needed to see why. She had never been enough for any man in her life, that's why she believed that sex was all she had to offer, the wilder the better. From very early on, she had also learned that the more she could satisfy them, the more she had them at her feet, even if just for a couple of hours.

You made me feel beautiful in Santa Monica, she said to Bill in her thoughts, while taking a break from the makeup, and walking to her closet, tracing her fingers over the dress she wore during their first meeting, the one she hadn't worn since. *You made me fall in love, and I didn't need this shit,* she told him from a distance, putting the dress aside and grabbing a refilled plate of cocaine. She quickly got her fix, snorting three thick lines in a row and smoked the fourth one rolled in a cigarette, not even enjoying it.

"That's what I've become," she said, touching the reflection of her face in the mirror. K had to finish her eyes. Vera was waiting for her.

* * *

BEFORE MEETING BILL, K's relationships had been blurred by drugs and alcohol, and she could barely remember how to undress for a man, how to move her body and arouse a man without it. She didn't even know how to engage in an interesting conversation without being high. She rarely remembered the details of what she had done the night before, and waking up with former partners was always a struggle until she either disappeared before they opened their eyes, or poured them a drink and fixed them a line on the kitchen table in order to bear each other's presence without embarrassment. It was like walking on Hollywood Boulevard at eight o'clock on a Saturday morning. It's wrong no matter what you are wearing and no matter why you are there.

Vera's story had brought her back to a reality in which nothing would ever change. Bill was just another selfish character looking for short-term pleasure and no intimacy, a free exit with a quick check out. The old "It has nothing to do with you, baby. It's just me, and this is not the right time" thing.

She wondered who the man she had fallen in love with truly was, because for a fleeting moment, Bill seemed to care about the person she was.

Meeting with Vera wasn't about the woman's alleged revelations. K had accepted the invite because she was high and hadn't thought it over; she wanted to punish Bill.

"Nothing will happen," she told herself. "I'm just going to have coffee and she'll do all the talking."

K parked on Gayley Ave, fixed her hair under a black wool beanie, and ran quickly through the pouring rain.

Vera wasn't there yet. "She'll be back in a minute," a waiter said about her boss, when K asked for Vera. "Sit anywhere you want, I'll bring you the menu." With jeans, boots, and a black leather jacket, she felt dark, tough, and powerful enough to threaten the enemy and fight the war.

The meeting place was a French-inspired café in Westwood, around the corner from UCLA. The Parisian fin de siècle décor was recreated with antiques and cast-iron chandeliers, small wooden round tables and ancient mirrors. It was that kind of old-fashioned European elegance that makes you want to smoke cigarettes and talk poetry, or drink champagne and kiss a stranger in the rain. The smell of buttery croissants and freshly brewed coffee was so strong that even her numbed nose could perceive it.

She waited at the first table by the window and sipped sparkling water. Her mouth was dry, and her lipstick had already faded. K always kept a book in her purse, so she opened Cohen's *Beautiful Losers,* and started reading page 98, where she had left off three nights before; she stumbled upon the Greek origins of the word apocalyptic—what is revealed when the woman's veil is lifted.

"I am just having coffee," she said, staring at the page. Words were already disappearing from her sight, and the wisdom of her favorite poet disappeared, too, leaving no trace or scent.

She didn't want to be there; she was finally becoming aware of what a stupid choice she had made, and it was too late to walk out. *It will be over soon*, she thought. *I am going to leave as soon as I can, and no one will ever know.*

Vera arrived. An artificially refined fifty-something strawberry blonde who made her big entrance in high heels and brown fur. She looked confident and entitled— her skin as white as porcelain. Vera gave her coat to the waiter and smiled at him with flirty gratitude. She took a drag from her cigarette, mounted into an ivory cigarette holder, and adjusted the leopard-skin shawl to better cover her artificially wrinkle-free neck.

"Hello there, nice to meet you," Vera said with a hoarse voice, a fake-lovely and reassuring smile. "Oh my God, you're so much more beautiful than I thought."

K listened to what she had to say with difficulty, since the woman whispered. K denied having an intimate connection to Bill, and pretended she did not know what Vera was talking about when she wished K all the happiness in the world with him.

"Don't be so defensive," Vera said, reaching for K's hand across the table, like she was her best friend. "I'm truly happy he found someone like you, instead of some kind of celebrity he can't handle anyway. You know, darling," she continued, playing sexy with the cigarette holder and touching her lips. "They would screw him over just for money or fame. I've lived here all my life, I know how Hollywood works."

"I really don't know what you are talking about," K said, making sure her hands were out of reach, calling the waiter for more coffee—not because she needed more caffeine but to have another presence at the table. "I just interviewed Bill once. I don't know him that well."

"Dear," Vera smiled, with the inquisitive tone of a CIA agent about to start the torture. "I've read your interview, and only a woman who's been in his bed could write such a piece. No offense to your writing, of course," she sneered, composing with her voice an acute sound, and touching the pink blonde of her hair. "I read some of your other works, and I think we have many things in common. Listen, I have a part-time position here if you are interested in more work."

Vera played her part very well. She continued the praise by saying that K truly seemed to care for him and she was sure she would give him the love and understanding he deserved. K was slowly starting to realize that the level of obsession Vera had for Bill had long crossed the threshold of sanity.

K had never learned how to clearly separate the naïveté of her feelings from the reality of facts. Somehow she wanted to find some truth in Vera's words and job offer, and when the meeting was over, she foolishly thought that the woman wouldn't be hard to dismiss. In her mind, she had finally cleared the field of jealousy, and she could continue with her new life without the couple.

It's a Question of Trust

"Rid of Me" by PJ Harvey

The days that followed the coffee date with Vera turned out to be much harder than K had expected. Her brother Alessio had returned to Italy, and communication with Bill had died. On the other hand, her communication with Vera seemed to be rapidly growing, to the point where K was bothered, if not scared, by it.

It was the beginning of December 1994.

For the third month, K's period was late. She wasn't surprised or anxious about it. She had other things on her mind. She didn't consider it a priority or anything to worry about.

K wasn't working a lot. She had quit the job at the press agency because they weren't paying her enough, and they weren't willing to help her grow professionally or raise her salary. The adventure had been interesting at the beginning, especially for some of the artists she had been able to interview, but she now needed to reach the next level, something that was not apparently part of the company policy, or simply not meant to happen. No matter how hard she seemed to be working to excel, regardless of her double life the small office on the Bronson Avenue wasn't comfortable anymore. K wanted more.

Not that she was in any position to be spoiled with money, since she desperately needed it to sustain her life force. She had sold every piece of jewelry she owned already, together with much of her clothing. That frustrating routine was making things even worse, not giving her the time to write and focus on her novel.

Her expensive using habits were becoming a major issue both for her bank account and her wrecked body, yet she couldn't take the agency anymore. She quit on a Monday morning when they denied the raise she had demanded and she realized that her daily tasks in that office were drifting very far away from writing.

"It wasn't bad, K," her boss smugly told her, after reading the last piece she had delivered, never giving her the satisfaction of a compliment. "But stop pretending you are a writer, that's not what we want. Where's the news here? You want the cover? Get the scoop! If you get me a photo of Tom Cruise cheating on Nicole Kidman, now we are talking money! But hey, if this is what you got, it's fine, too, I guess," he continued, throwing the piece of paper on the desk with the arrogance of someone with experience in the field of international journalism. "Let's see what the editor says."

The article K had been working on for days was never published. Apparently, gossip was a major concern for the team. And, even though K's timing had never been appropriate in life, both in her professional and personal history, writing photo captions on the brand new red carpet outfits was not her cup of tea.

Without a regular job, she barely had the money to survive. She had reached that place again, that place of misery.

Every time she got loaded, she promised her grandmother and God that it would be the last time, if only they would show her a sign. It had become a ritual on the bathroom floor, but the sign was never sent, or she never saw it.

She was not working on her book any more. Twenty-four hours were not enough to silence her brain, pour vodka in her coffee or in her evening canned soup (that is what she could afford by then—also a good way to hide the abnormal quantity of alcohol she had gotten used to).

K hallucinated ants under her skin and became more and more paranoid. The high fever was ordinary, and she lived in fear of getting caught by the police everywhere she went, even if it was just around the block to get coffee or cigarettes, with the risk of being sent not to jail, but back to Italy, since they had the power of revoking her already-precarious visa. The only time she would go out was to replace the bottles of vodka and wine she drank, buy cigarettes and a blueberry muffin at the gas station around the corner, or gather the money she owed her several dealers. They were nice guys though, and they delivered, too, almost 24/7.

People started to leave her behind. She desperately held onto any conversation and human contact she could. Sex was something she could barely remember, the last of her priorities. That's why the frequent phone calls from Vera made her feel part of something, of a world that had forgotten about her struggle, but that kept spinning, with or without K. She wasn't the victim people loved to take care of anymore. There was no father to get attention from, no mother to punish and emulate, no man to impress with her sexual skills, and no brother to avoid, ignore, and compete with.

She was alone. Few people knew how far she had fallen, and the few who did were tired of helping her. Not even her therapist had faith in K anymore. She was a lost cause at that point, and Vera was penetrating that thick brick wall. The more the woman reached for her, the more she felt worthy of her presence in her life.

"My kid's life was in danger," Bill explained, almost feeling guilty for not being able to be a good father. "I had to erase K from my life at that point, Angie," he later told me in tears.

K hadn't mentioned what happened. I tried to dig deeper, without forcing his hand, because I could see not only his pain, but for the first time his embarrassment, and that vulnerability K had witnessed in his sickness.

"Because what Vera did was so perverse, even K thought it was too much to handle," he said, without even looking me in the eye. "I had to protect my son and my family at that point. K wasn't part of it. I am not saying I did the right thing, but at that time it was the only way out I could see."

After two weeks of correspondence, Vera had fired the bullet and finally put her finely orchestrated plan in action.

It was a late night when K received a phone call from Bill, after ages of silence. Apparently the woman had been following them, hacking phone calls, telling lies to all of Bill's friends and family, and obsessing over public mentions of him, while using every piece of information she could get to attack. That's how she tracked K down in first place. Needless to say, K never felt more naive; she was the cause of all the pain that came. She was the reason why Bill had ignored her, for by being a source of information to Vera, she was dangerous for him and his son.

The restaurant manager had apparently planned it all from the very beginning, and K had to admit defeat. Vera had reached her goal and Bill had to protect his family by cutting off any possible link with his ex, and at that point, K was a very tight and dangerous one. She had lost her position in his life. She was now just another sick woman trying to complicate his self-centered and precarious existence.

"I asked you to refrain from getting involved, K," Bill told her during a late-night phone call—4:30 a.m.—cold as ice, like he barely knew her. "But no, you needed to prove you were smarter, didn't you? You didn't trust me, you had to see who she was, right?"

"I am sorry, Bill," K apologized. She was still unaware of what he was about to do. "I had no idea, and I have never told her about us or about you. Why didn't you tell me how really dangerous she was? I've made a mistake, but I cut her out Bill, I promise," she begged.

"You should have just trusted my words, without any further explanation. She stole a bunch of money from my bank account. I don't even know how she got the phone records. From what I know, you are still sharing everything with her. You have no idea what you have just put yourself into. But, at this point," Bill continued, "my family comes first. You jeopardized the safety and sanity of my own son. He's been through enough shit already.

"Maybe you and my ex can commiserate." He ended the conversation and hung up the phone.

It was the last time she heard from him for a long time, no matter how hard she tried to apologize to make him understand who she really was, and that she had never been part of any plan to hurt him or his family. An endless list of handwritten letters, gifts, confessions, concerns, and cries for help, nothing ever worked.

It was the beginning of the end.

Having finished all the drugs she could afford that day, and probably that week, she searched in vain for money in her wallet. Ten dollars was all she could find. She looked at herself in the living room mirror, the one hanging on the so-called "wall of love," according to Carrie's feng shui creed, and she cried all her tears, hating herself with every particle still alive in her body.

Her second drink didn't help. She washed her face and opened the bathroom cabinet. Her mother had just sent her a present from Italy, and seven boxes of Xanax were fortunately part of it.

Her hands were shaking and sweat ran like a river down her face. She needed something stronger, but her dealer wouldn't give her a thing for free, and she did not have anyone to borrow money from at that point. Those pills were her only chance to get through the night, hoping for a better score the following day. She just wanted to sleep.

She felt empty and overwhelmed. She hurt at the thought that Bill couldn't see what she was doing to herself. Before blacking out on the couch in a living room that smelled of weed and French fries, she hated him like she had never hated anyone before, not even Marco.

He just proved me right, K thought before closing her eyes. *The only thing I am good at is sex. He never gave me a chance. At least Marco knew who I really was.* She got up from the couch to look at her face in the mirror one more time, just to make sure she was really the same old K. Bill couldn't be right, she was a good person, she didn't want to hurt anyone. *Men did use me. But some of them made the effort, at least. Bill doesn't even bother.* And she lapsed back on the couch, paralyzed.

She seized the bottle of Xanax with tears in her eyes and sweat in her hands, slowly opened it, and one by one she swallowed the pills, five of them, to survive the night and forget what she had done. Many were the days and the nights that the medication had already deleted from her memory. She prayed for that one to become one of them.

It's Either Life or Death

"Pennyroyal Tea" by Nirvana

She could smell it in the air.

The smell of death had never been so penetrating and difficult to hide on K's neck. She was alone in the apartment. Carrie was in Vegas with friends for a birthday party.

It was precisely one week after Bill's phone call, when K deliberately tried to overdose with what she had at her disposal.

She couldn't put an end to her existence made of clouds and of a pursuit of some kind of peace. So she had run to the safest place she knew and let fate decide. But she planned it, in every single detail. She decided to indulge in it until the end came in her candlelight bedroom carefully decorated for the occasion.

Before the night arrived, she took a hot shower and sprayed lavender oil on her body. Her skin was dry. She had not been showering regularly lately. She wanted to be at her most beautiful for the special occasion, for when they would find her. She had failed years before; this time everything had to be perfect. Since it was early in the afternoon, she cleaned her closet before starting the death party. She also straightened up the bedroom and burned patchouli essential oil, because she wanted to have an intense smell to remember, while slowly fading away. When the cleaning and beautifying process was completed, she turned the music on in the living room and made herself a perfect martini cocktail, with olive and lemon essence. She was going too far too soon with cocaine and she needed a break. Heroin was the special dessert for the after dinner. She still had to make a gourmet meal, and she did not want to skip the pleasure part of her death plan. She took some Xanax with her cocktail, allowed her heart to slow down in beats and started cooking with the best ingredients she could find at Mrs. Gooch's.

K allowed her mouth and her senses to enjoy a proper meal, the first one in ages. Not that she was hungry, but she had to force her body. She had been starving herself for so many years that she did not want to die a bulimic. She had set the table almost like she was waiting for her man to arrive from work, with red roses in one hand, and a Marlboro red in the other. Wine was on the house, a very special one, for a very special evening.

Surprisingly, she did not think about Bill, other than at the end of the night, for a final farewell. And when she pictured a man by her side that night, his lines were very close to the charming photographer she had dated when

Bill cut her off, more to prove to herself that she could live without him, than to actually give the nice guy a chance.

The imaginary man was wearing old blue jeans with a dark brown leather belt and a black shirt. His hair was messy, a lovely shade of ash blond.

She barely touched the food, of course, but she went through the whole dinner without regrets, dessert included. It was vanilla bean ice cream with homemade strawberry sauce, from an old recipe her mother had given her, just in case she had to make an Italian meal for her new American friends. Like K really had any, apart from Carrie.

She drank some wine, the expensive kind she had been saving for the occasion, and played Nirvana's *MTV Unplugged in New York*, before heading to the bathroom, where the after-party was scheduled to continue.

The toxic mix was already having the desired effect, and quicker than she thought. In her previous life, she could have been a scientist—hallucinations came very soon. They were not frightening that night—LAPD and helicopters were not involved. But Kurt Cobain was. She had always loved and relied on his music, and his struggle couldn't have been more familiar to her. He was there, next to K, on air from the turntable, or from the afterworld. She saw him by her side. There must have been a reason why he was there in such a peculiar circumstance, and she couldn't think about anything but the ugly and simple truth: he had already walked that narrow sea, and lost his battle just a few months earlier. He had fallen to the ground alone, and alone he had died. He had fallen right where she was losing the last bit of a balance. Kurt was there, and he was the only familiar presence in that house. He had spent hours watching from far away; always ready to take K into his arms, when the time would come for her to finally let go.

For a millisecond she felt like the Hollywood apartment she had moved into with Carrie was a private Rock and Roll Hall of Fame, but she soon realized that it was just a cemetery of wasted talent and silent pain. Beverlywood, her very first apartment in Los Angeles, was a distant memory, as far in space and time as all the remaining reminiscences of her life.

K sensed the beauty that was never enough, regardless of how elegant the lace dress was, or how perfect the necklace sat on her skin. She allowed the sadness and disappointment to be and then forgave herself for what she had done and for what she was about to do. She cuddled the reflection of what she saw with self-pity and the beginning of love. She was a woman about to die. Kurt's peaceful smile stood patient and serene next to her.

"Something in the Way" played. She sat down on the floor, by the bathtub, heated up the tiny aluminum foil with a white round candle she was holding between her legs, and inhaled from the thin, silvery tube she had already prepared, because everything had to be perfect for the last night. She inhaled the vapor, deeper and deeper, trying not to burn herself or waste that little chunk of black tar she had bought to celebrate her death. She was impatiently waiting for the kick. But the high wasn't exactly what she had hoped for. She wasn't in a hurry. K knew this moment would come, when she needed more and more again. She had some more and burned it all, hoping in vain to go back to the very first high.

"It's my choice," she thought out loud, talking to her personal Jesus in heaven, that one who had never listened to any of her prayers. "No one is here to save me. Kurt is ready to catch me, and he will walk with me through the shift."

She was alone. And her sanity had long gone.

She thought about calling Bill to rescue her, but he would never pick up the phone, and a rejection would only complicate her death plan. So she said goodbye to him, in between smokes.

Hours passed by. And the end walked towards her, closer and closer. K was impatient, craving silence, so Kurt's sweet voice had to stop her from hurrying up the journey.

It's the last one, he said. *Don't waste it, you will cry no more tomorrow.*

I promise. I can't wait to meet you there, we will sing eternally.

Those images were so vivid in her diary that if I didn't know Kurt Cobain had already died, I wouldn't believe it was just a hallucination.

Kurt's voice was The One, and she couldn't help but listen to it, as you might do with your god of choice.

Kurt was the holy book, K's holy hope that night. When the effect of the toxic smoke in the bathroom wrapped her body in a chemical blanket, it was time for the final rest. She took the Xanax, well aware of the effect it would produce combined with the cocaine. Somehow Kurt guided her through the entire ritual; from the very first step until the very last breath, when she fell asleep and thought she was finally dead.

When Carrie found her on the floor, the day after, and woke her up, K could not put words together or remember what had happened. She refused to go to the ER because she did not have medical insurance. They would find drugs in her system and she could lose her visa. Carrie took care of her at home. As soon as her condition got better, the fever had lowered down and she was able to talk, the only thing she could recall was that she wasn't scared. Kurt Cobain made her feel safe, not like a hopeless, breathing mistake of nature anymore.

My blood decorated flowers on the wooden floor, so creative in its desperation to escape the veins.

How beautiful. I could taste it and it didn't hurt…it was happening exactly how I had planned it in my dreams, she wrote, unaware that someone would read her words at this point, but simply determined to find a reason why she was still alive. *I had tried to kill myself, again.*

Water ran to clean the sink and eliminate the proof. But apart from water and Nirvana, I could only hear tear drops on the broken pocket mirror, and blood, too, staining the surface on a cold California winter. Tic-tac, tic-tac; the drops knocked on the surface like marking time. Then, shortly before I closed my eyes for what I thought was forever, the music faded, too.

There was a moment when I hesitated, she confessed, *but Kurt took my hand in his. He gathered my hair in a ponytail, just like my mother used to do when I was a little girl.*

One last smoke, no men existed anymore, no family, and no guilt. My past disappeared. My birth even erased from the history books. And dinner so far away that I completely forgot the food I had. My body had lost its weight.

I remembered the wine, but not its smell.

He held my hand in the bathroom. Step-by-step; line-by-line; drop-by-drop. And then he kissed me. He licked the blood on my lower lips and carried me to the bed in the other room.

Candles burned all night long. But not when I woke up.

He closed my eyes with his fingers and kept holding my hand until my body was dead cold.

I thought I was dead, Carrie. She broke into tears. *I don't know why I'm still alive, again.*

You need to rest now, sweetheart, Carrie said, holding her hand. She helped her drink some water.

I know you think I'm crazy, K said. Her voice was feeble, and yet determined at the same time, *but I don't want to die anymore, Carrie. I'm done with this. I promise.* She broke into tears again. *I'm getting sober.*

* * *

WHEN K FOUND OUT she was pregnant, her whole world fell apart again. She had been late so many times given her physical condition that she had never even worried about it before. She did not want a child. She was too weak to be a mother, barely able to walk by herself.

Two days after waking up in her Hollywood bedroom, she decided to surrender and went to an AA meeting. It was a cold Tuesday night. And it was the first step towards the new shape of a woman she was about to discover and embrace.

Still struggling to get up every morning and to try and live what everybody else called life, she managed to start walking again, on her own. Very slowly, and with the priceless, unconditional help of the new friends who were guiding her through the process, she had started to show some willingness. Old friends had disappeared anyway. They were either fake or just tired, hurt too deeply by K's actions and selfishness.

While working on admitting that she was powerless, she remembered the conversation she had had with Bill on the terrace at the Chateau Marmont. Her life had become unmanageable and she had reached her bottom. She started to drink more tea and also reopened the novel—tentatively titled *The Sex Girl*. In that moment, she became aware of how much both thoughts and feelings could wound her if not transformed into words. The turning around Bill had promised started to make more sense. That's why she used the paper: to find some peace, or redemption.

How am I going to do this sober? she thought on the first day of work. But that's when more of his words came to mind, and she realized he would never set her free. The baby was six weeks old.

"It's when the chair gets uncomfortable, K, when writing makes you squirm, that's the challenge finally worth experiencing and actually remembering," he told her while sharing his past of heroin, writing, and lies. "For years I thought I could never write a line without drugs," he confessed. "But it's when I got clean that I finally realized that being fucked up was just an excuse. It takes balls to write the truth."

Since she had quit her underpaid job as a journalist, she looked for another one to pay off her debts, and luckily enough Carrie was still by her side, and helped her as much as she could. She realized that true friendship was not a matter of years of companionship, but a gift that you can find at your doorstep when you least expect it. Through Carrie, K had found a part-time job in a clothing store in Hollywood, not far from where she lived. It was not her cup of tea, but it gave her enough money to pay rent, and helped her to experience a world that K had completely forgotten existed.

The timing, however, was terrible for motherhood—Bill was obviously the wrong man.

He was old and already had a fourteen-year-old son. His health wasn't stable enough. But most of all, he did not want more kids. How was that new life supposed to grow up with a father like him, and with a mother who, somehow, was still a child herself?

How am I supposed to tell him? She thought, not even able to start the conversation with Carrie.

After what they had done to each other, she couldn't imagine what his reaction would be. He had abandoned K, never trusting the candor of her feelings. Bill never understood how much she cared for him. His old ways were more powerful than what they could have had. She started questioning every word and every moment; Bill had not been able to forgive. *Is he even capable of love?* she wrote.

What if this child is just another mistake for him? she asked herself over and over again.

K had tried everything that was in her power to apologize and repair the damage, but he had shut her out completely, and left no room for negotiation. He had ignored her when she had needed him the most; he had decided to live life his own way and he surely did not want another family or another partner to possibly cheat on.

Half of her heart loved the unborn life already, but the other one was wrestling with the overwhelming feeling of the unwanted gift. There was no easy escape. She had to tell him, and only then, to do the right thing for her and the baby.

K spent long nights trying to find the courage to call Bill, as only Carrie knew about the pregnancy. She had not been praying lately either; it took time to get into that habit and establishing an honest, selfless connection with the higher unknown she had been used to hating and blaming for her suffering.

The Old Diner, the New Life

"Everything in its Right Place" by Radiohead

They say to be careful what you wish for, because you might get it, and that's exactly what happened to K.

In January of 1995, she was stabilizing: thirty days sober and ten weeks pregnant, although you could barely see it, given her recovering body frame. She was finally on the right path. K was discovering a life she had never dreamed of, a power she did not know she owned, some kind of faith, and an inner strength that was helping her to stay sober, to fit into the world.

"I'm really proud of you," Carrie told her, pointing at the white thirty-day chip on the kitchen table, where they were having tea, just the two of them, like the old times. "I know that it didn't work with him, but he needs to know. Regardless of what he decides. He is the father."

Life wasn't always easy for bubbly Carrie, but she had the power of turning every drama into something easy to deal with. Carrie believed in magic and astrological signs, she lived her life with the moon by her side, always careful not to start a new project or an important conversation when Mercury was in retrograde. She was a witch, a powder fairy with colorful jewelry and bizarre religious views. She relied on alternative energies and didn't like politics, but she always tried to do the right thing for the people she cared for. Everything was always possible in Carrie's eyes, no matter how old you were and how many times you had tried.

"Blondie," K tried to explain, holding the chip tight in her hands like it was her talisman. "Do you want the truth? I miss him. Every day. You know how much it hurts to see him at the gym and be ignored when he pretends he doesn't even know me?" she confessed, ashamed to admit that such a passionate affair had turned out to be nothing more than indifference. "I am so scared of facing him that when I see his car in the parking lot I run away. I can't deal with the embarrassment and the hurt of him not even saying, "Hi." How am I supposed to tell him that I am pregnant with his child?" A tear came down. "I don't know what to do. This time is different. He's not coming back."

She had slowly gotten used to life without him. But Bill was about to walk onto the stage again, and in such a humble way that K could not help but respond to it.

As usual, Bill used his art, his words. He sent K the most unexpected, sweet and humble letter of amends she could ever expect from him.

What I did was unfair, K. She could read his sorrow between the lines; she could read the truth and the beauty of his chosen loneliness, and his embarrassment, too, for what had happened. *Because of the toxic craziness with Vera,* the letter continued, *which had profoundly fucked up ramifications, I associated you with that situation. It scared me. But I shouldn't have treated you the way I did. I know you did not intentionally participate in anything destructive, and I know you truly care.*

K was still in the dark about what Vera had done, but Bill seemed to have realized what kind of woman K was. For the first time, this letter ended with *Love, Bill.*

It was early in the morning when K read the letter, and morning sickness was still kicking in heavy. When he had come back the first time, months before, she was ready for the adventure. But now, she was pregnant with his kid and in no position to be hurt again. She couldn't afford to relapse.

K's doctor had been extremely clear a couple of weeks earlier, when Carrie took her to the hospital, for the routine visit.

"You're alive," the doctor said, while helping K to sit in the sterile elegance of his Brentwood studio. "It's already a miracle. I hope you realize that."

"This pregnancy," he continued, "is something that I can barely explain myself. Your heart and kidneys suffered some major damage, and your body barely has enough nutrients to feed you both right now. You need to be very careful, K."

"What are the chances?" she asked, not exactly sure what she was hoping to hear. "What should I do? What are the risks?"

"Well," he said with a voice more serious than one she could recall hearing since that day in the principal's office, back in high school, when she was caught smoking pot in the boys' locker room. "How much do you want to survive this, and how much do you care about this child? If you want to be a mother you must be ready to make some major changes. If you don't, both your life and the baby's will be in danger." He took his glasses off, just like you see in the movies. "I am serious, K. This is your choice and only yours. Do you know who the father is? I haven't seen anyone with you."

"Of course I do," K replied embarrassed and bothered by the question at the same time—*Who the hell is this man to judge me?*

"Well, I'd talk to him if I were you. You will need a lot of help. You can't do this alone. I am going to see you in two weeks," he wrote K a prescription and helped her to the door.

"Thank you, Doctor. I have friends, but I appreciate your concern. I'll see you in two weeks."

As if K didn't have enough storms to avoid and deal with, she couldn't stop thinking about Bill's note; he had finally realized who she was and had opened up again. Bill had apologized and in those few lines, she felt that he had also changed somehow. She called him later that same night and they decided to meet for coffee over the weekend. K had to tell him what was going on.

This time K chose the place. She did not feel comfortable meeting him at his house. She did not feel safe there. So they agreed on Canter's.

Contrasting feelings battled in her mind: fear, remorse, hope. She was not sure how he would react to the news of a baby. It was the last thing they both wanted, but they were adults, and they would deal with it, one way or another.

The time was set for five in the afternoon, and she had the entire day to prepare a speech, finish an article for a local music magazine that had hired her part-time to interview the new rising talents of the underground Los Angeles music scene, go for a quick relaxing walk, take a shower, and decide what to wear for the soon-to-be father of her child.

Just a cigarette—she hadn't smoked one since the day the test had turned out positive, in the restroom of CVS, right after buying it.

She knew smoking wasn't part of the pregnancy program, but just once, a Marlboro Light she had gotten from Carrie was allowed. The Bill occasion required it. She did not smoke the entire cigarette; it would be her last one.

It was still early, so she parked two blocks away from the deli and walked, daydreaming about what would happen next. These were the last fragments of her old life. From that day on, everything would be different.

When I read this part of the journal, I couldn't stop crying. K really tried to change and become a woman, and whether Bill would be by her side or not, she fought to stay sober and give her child and herself a real life. For the first time, she was learning how to live in the real world without the mask, accepting the consequences of her nature, of what she had done. And this time no one had asked her to do it: She was the one working for it. K had stopped digging.

There were times when she missed drugs, how everything disappeared with liquor; she missed the feeling of being sick, the thin, dying teenager in need of rescue. K still felt like an alien without it.

Life does not get better. We get better at dealing with it. In that same moment she knew that no matter what Bill's reaction was, she was absolutely sure about what she was going to do, and she was ready to deal with it.

When she walked into the diner, Bill was already there, waiting for her at the last hidden table by the wall, the one in the right corner of the main room. He looked like he could feel that something was about to happen, his face partially darkened by the big menu. He glowed unusually.

Can he possibly know? K thought, quickly, while slowly making her way to the table. *I haven't gained weight, I didn't mention anything on the phone and Carrie is the only one who knows. No, he doesn't know. I'm just being paranoid,* she said to herself, while pretending to fix her ponytail. *Breathe, K, just breathe.* And she was there, in front him, again.

When K got close to the table, Bill stood up, less self-confident than usual. He brushed his fingers against her cheek, almost afraid of hurting her, and they both took their seat on the red leather, just opposite the booth of their Greek-salad-and-strawberry-cheesecake date.

"You look great," Bill said. "I still wonder why you keep wanting to see me." He touched her hand just like he used to do when he wanted to have sex. "But hey, I'm not complaining. Actually, you look beautiful."

"Thank you," K said, not really playing the game this time. "It might be sobriety."

"Wow, that's a surprise, I am proud of you. You know, I am just an old Jew trying to write another novel, but getting sober was the best thing I've ever done for myself. What made you change your mind?"

"It's a long story but…I need to talk to you…" K nervously changed the topic when the waiter interrupted them to take the order.

It took just a couple of minutes. Like every time they had dined at Canter's, they knew exactly what they wanted—matzo ball soup for her and the smoked salmon plate for him. They both ordered some tea and politely got rid of their waiter. After placing the order, she put down the pickle she was torturing with her teeth, and not really enjoying, and looked him in the eyes. She could not wait any longer. The shocking words came out of her mouth just like the "I love you" on the way to San Francisco in the dirty motel:

"I know we have other issues to discuss, but there's something that comes first, Bill."

"What's wrong?"

"I…I am pregnant."

Silence.

Later, she described the scene in such a detailed way that I was there with them, right when the secret was being revealed at Canter's, on that chilly Los Angeles afternoon. He stood up to change his seat and sat next to her.

Silence, still.

They did not move for a while, almost afraid to talk or even to breathe. A long silence took over and she did not know what to expect. Bill was not an easy man to understand, and he was not sending signals of any kind.

After a couple of minutes that seemed to be hours, he took her in his arms and she surrendered her head to his chest, but they didn't say a word. He kissed her hair, touched her face with his lips and, only then, whispered in her ears, more because he didn't want to be heard by the rest of the people eating next to them than to actually embody the husband/dad-to-be.

"You are pregnant," he repeated, shocked but tender at the same time. "You are pregnant," he said again to make sure he had understood correctly. "Is that why you got sober?"

"No," K said, not really eager to discuss sobriety in that particular moment, but more interested in the *What are we going to do next?* part. *I almost died, if you really want to know the truth,* she wanted to tell him. "I didn't even know I was pregnant when I blacked out, overdosed or whatever happened. It is a miracle, the doctor said."

He kept staring at her in silence, torturing his curly, silver hair that needed styling. His face was still in shock as he thought about the right thing to say and do, not in the next ten years but right then, in the next ten seconds.

"K," he whispered. "I didn't even know I could still have kids with this treatment I am having. How's that possible?"

"Well, I didn't know I could get pregnant, Bill, because of my weight and how much I was using," she confessed. "I was barely having my periods. When I found out, I didn't know what to do. I know you don't want more kids, and I'm obviously not ready to have one. That's why I waited to tell you. You are free Bill, to walk away from this." She sipped from her cup and attempted to relax the muscles on her face. Her eyes reflected courage straight into his, and she was ready for the verdict. K had grown up all of a sudden. "You know I love you, but this is not what I wanted. You deserved to know, but I don't want your money and I don't want you, if you don't want this." She took a deep breath, the hard part was about to be over. "I wanted to tell you the truth and I wanted to tell you that I never meant to hurt you. Please," she continued, grabbing her purse and car keys from the table, "don't make a decision now. It wouldn't be wise. This isn't about you and me. Call me, and we can talk it over, decide what to do next."

"You have barely touched your soup," he said. "Why don't you stay a little longer?"

"You need some time, Bill," her hand sweetly on his shoulder. "I am not going anywhere, this is serious. You can't change your mind this time. You don't have to choose me. You just have to decide if you want to be in the baby's life. That's all I want to know."

"K, sit down. I don't have to think about it. I don't know if I can have a relationship now, I know I'm not the father you want for your kid, but, that said, I won't make the same mistakes I have made in the past. I want to be the father to our baby."

"Bill," K said after a long silence, not even able to cry at that point. "Are you sure? I mean, I'm beyond happy, and I don't care if you don't want to be with me any more," she lied, "but…are you really sure?"

"I fucked up with my son, K." The guilt was palpable. "I missed everything of his childhood, and I caused such an excruciating pain in his life that I still ask myself how he can call me Dad. I love him to death." Still, the regret and the self-loathing echoed in his voice as he played with the almost untouched food, just like a kid. "Maybe this is my chance to redeem myself and hold a newborn without worrying about blood and track marks on my arms, actually remember it. Yes, I am sure, K."

The scenario wasn't the most desirable: Bill was fifty-seven and did not want a relationship. He was about to have a baby with a then twenty-five-year-old woman, a little over a month sober and recovering from a life of bulimia.

* * *

"Wednesday Morning, 3 A.M." by Simon & Garfunkel

THE DAY AFTER THE confession she decided to treat herself to the luxury of a shopping day in Santa Monica.

Shopping had been so rare for K that she always marked it on the calendar. After almost an hour of looking for parking, she was so tired that she walked into the first cafe she saw for a rest and lunch.

She allowed herself something more than canned tuna, and it warmed my heart to read her words of hope when she was pregnant, truly believing in a rebirth. I guess the unborn child gave K the courage to start rebuilding her entire existence from scratch. It felt like watching a baby learning how to walk, how to speak, how to eat, how to shower and perceive her body. The vulnerability I read through K's honest confession was at once moving and sour.

What am I doing here? she thought, while waiting in line for her lunch, realizing that she was about to raise a baby in Los Angeles, far from her roots, with Bill's shitty health insurance. Still, she would never return to Italy. She loved America. It had believed in her talent and given her a chance. Against all odds, Los Angeles had also grown inside her. As much as she knew that travels would be part of her professional future, both her and Bill's life would be based in Southern California—the place she had now started to call home.

The unreasonable number of people waiting in line made her realize that she was not in the mood for a day of waiting, especially for couple of T-shirts and a pair of shoes she didn't even need. So, after lunch, she walked the ocean barefoot and inhaled it deeply, with wet sand on her feet and salty tears of gratitude in her eyes.

If I only knew eight years ago that the ocean had this power, she thought, smiling at the waves. Every thought moved across her mind like lines of poetry across the page. The more I read, the more I felt like I was secretly watching K through a hidden mirror.

Bill had never lied—even with a baby on the way, he had a lot on his plate, and a real relationship was not something he was sure he could offer her. The fact that she had accepted their new arrangement with an inner hope for more was something she had to deal with by herself.

Bill's health was getting worse, the medications he was taking for his Hepatitis C were heavy, *but not in a good way,* he used to say, relying on his humor to survive. The side effects were devastating on both his body and his brain. That was why they rarely went out and spent most of the time at his house. Even though the drive up the hill wasn't the best thing for K's broken Camaro, she could never get enough of the view from the terrace, where everything had started and from where everything still seemed perfect. At Bill's, she could admire the outside world without participating in it.

The nights spent at his house became more and more frequent, and K's body became curvier every day. They were both sober. They were both real. And they were in it together.

Her body was creating life; Bill touched it with his unintentionally grateful hands and she didn't need drugs or alcohol or masks to forget what it meant to be.

What was not supposed to be a relationship slowly became a family when K silently moved into Bill's house, five months pregnant.

K knew what the danger was, the high-risk situation she had put herself into again. She wondered if that higher power of hers would send the same lesson until she finally got it. But K was trying to avoid paranoia, she would analyze the lesson another day.

What if I'm just becoming stronger? She thought, while washing her face, in his luxurious bathroom, just behind the bedroom. *What if that's the lesson I have to learn this time?* She turned the lights off and went back to bed where he was waiting for her, reading a book, with his dark-framed glasses on.

"I know this isn't what you were looking for," she whispered, putting the book down, and taking his glasses off. "I didn't want this either, trust me," she continued. "Not with a baby, not like this."

"Sometimes you just get what you need, baby." His kisses had become more genuine since she had moved in. Bill was falling in love, even though he never told her. He never would. He kissed her again and couldn't stop staring at her body next to his, like a miracle or some kind of curse. "Keith has always been one of my heroes; everything's going to be fine. We'll work this out. I promise. And you'll be ninety days tomorrow. It's a big chip!"

She fell asleep, temporarily reassured, resting on his chest, while he continued to read *For Whom The Bell Tolls.*

Maybe Keith Richards was right: he had made their same mistakes and he was still alive.

If she only knew what was ahead. If only she could read the end of her own story.

Ashes to ashes.

Nine months passed and, in another form, she was born again.

Let Me Introduce Myself

"Angie" by The Rolling Stones

The day I was born, my mother died.

My name is Angie, and the day I was born, seventeen years ago, K died.

"Aneurysm," the medical report read. And when they took her to the hospital, there was nothing the doctors could do to save her. She tried to hang on to life, fight fate, but only a few minutes after my first breath, her heart stopped beating. Bill was there. He could not believe what he had just lost. Years later, he confessed that he could not take me into his arms, but only stare at K's dead body. He did not cry. Not visible tears, at least. Denial was apparently the only remedy on hand in that moment. He wanted to hold a newborn in his arms without heroin, but without heroin he experienced grief.

"It was her choice," the memory still hurt like he had lost her the day before. I stood before him, his own daughter, his murmur mine, too, while I listened. "Her choice. Jesus Christ! She didn't want a hospital and she didn't want anesthesia. She was in that pink cloud of sober life and anesthesia scared her to death."

"What did it have to do with drugs?"

"For your mother, there was no in-between in life, and since she had gotten sober she had decided that her approach to life would change, too, starting with you. The doctor tried to stop her from going to the midwife, but K was stubborn and did not follow his advice. She wanted the best for you, she wanted to feel the pain and remember the emotion of giving birth. She wanted to be surrounded by familiar images, and not by sterile bed sheets and Jell-O in a plastic cup. The house, can you believe that? In the hills...far from everything, I was so stupid to say yes."

I recall that day, when he finally revealed the story. That day I saw my father cry for the first time. He poured some tea and turned the radio off. We were listening to some political talk radio. Those talks helped him write, or so he said.

"That's where she gave birth to you." He knew he couldn't stop the story from being told at that point. "With Paula, the midwife that had been following the pregnancy from the very beginning, together with her first doctor. Bradley method," he said, ready to spit the truth and let go of the rage.

"That's how I was born?"

"Your mother was an extremist," he justified, trying to give K's choice a meaning, while walking towards the kitchen window, avoiding my eyes. "And, after years of pumping poison into her body, she firmly believed that you deserved the purest version of her. She refused any kind of anesthesia or medication, even though it was highly recommended, given her health conditions. It was black or white. She was either a sinner or a saint."

"Was she healed?" I asked, to have a truth to believe in, to feel reassured or maybe just to stop blaming myself for her death.

"From drugs? Yes. From the voice inside her head? Never. We never do, Angie."

He was a man still grieving. With K he had tried to give love a try, and the loss had devastated him. They were never meant to be together. It was fate. K's past was well known to both my father and her doctors, yet apparently an old gastrointestinal surgery she underwent when she was nineteen had remained unknown to them all.

"Copper deficiency," he said, cold as ice, just like reading from a medical dictionary. "It's a rare disease that can be caused by such surgical procedures, especially when connected to bulimia. Aneurysm is one of the main causes of death, no matter how young you are."

"Did Paula take care of me then when I was born?"

"She did, while I called nine-one-one and her doctor. She was unconscious but still alive, but by the time they took her to the hospital, there was nothing they could do to save her." He wanted me to know that K loved me.

And that is why he told me the truth, even though he had his doubts. "The doctor also explained to me that there were very few chances they could have performed any procedure to save K because of the nature of the aneurysm, so at this point," he hesitated, still avoiding my face, "I don't really know how much her choice really mattered."

Only after covering my mother with a white sheet did he call the nurse and ask about me. They had not decided my name yet, but they were both fans of the Stones. K's favorite song was "Angie."

I was born Angie Werber on a sunny and windy day of July in 1995, on the eastern hills of Los Angeles, in my father's house, free from drugs and alcohol, the healthiest baby they had ever seen. K's body was strong enough to carry and nourish me, but it wasn't able to save her and let her survive. Her life gifted her with me, and punished her at the same time.

K died at the age of twenty-five.

She was beautiful and she was strong.

She was smart and she was brave.

She made mistakes and she paid for them.

She started loving herself when it was too late. She loved herself when she started loving me.

* * *

LIFE WITH BILL AS a father wasn't easy. As K had anticipated, we traveled a lot. But as much as he wanted to leave Los Angeles, his life was there and we ended up flying back and forth between the coasts.

A couple of times he took me to Italy to visit my grandparents, but over the years, we spent much of our time in New York. He had bought an apartment on Charles Street, in the West Village, many years before, right after his second novel was made into a successful movie, *Darkness Within*. And he had many friends there, his yoga teacher, too. Yoga was just one of the many practices that was helping him survive, sober, and with the precarious inner balance he had built over time. He had nailed it to a severe perfection, which allowed him to take care of me and keep working with words. Bill wasn't different from K. His struggle never ended, either.

He never made me feel like I was a mistake, but I know the truth—he didn't want another kid. When I was fourteen, he gave me K's diary. He had never read it before but on the day she died, he wrote "THE END" on what he thought would become her great first novel. The diary became my Bible for the four years to come. And for as much as I could feel Bill's love and good intentions, I have never been able to ignore the fact that I was the result of a mistake, of a fight on the stairs when he didn't want her there. I was the result of two struggling souls loving each other and trying to get by the best way they could.

Today we are free, my mother and I, at least.
We make mistakes, over and over again.
We give in. We lie.
We dwell into our pain because it looks easier than accepting happiness.
Nevertheless, there comes a time when we have the chance to stand up, start all over.
Yes, we do make mistakes.
We give in and we lie.
We are not perfect. But the bravest step we can take is making our amends; forgive who must be forgiven and turn the page.
That is the most powerful sign of love we can offer.
Until then, until we realize that, we slowly and painfully die inside.
In this diary I am making amends, I am forgiving who must be forgiven and I am starting over.
—From K's diary. She was ten days sober.

They keep asking me why I wasn't able to stop.
I still don't have the answer.
The only thing I do know is that I had to die, to be reborn.
It was the hardest thing I ever did in my whole life.

THE END

Message From the Author

This story is a work of fiction. In the eighties and nineties—when K struggled with eating disorders, alcoholism, addiction, and self-harm—the Internet wasn't popular, if available at all.

Today, more and more women and men suffer from bulimia, anorexia, alcoholism, and addiction.

I am Alice Carbone, the author of this novel. I am a recovering bulimic and alcoholic. These diseases have ruined years of my life, and almost killed me.

During my struggle, the Internet made it worse, because of websites that promoted many of the above as a lifestyle. It took me a long time to understand that it was a lie, that I was hurting myself, and the people who loved me.

I am blessed to be here and to live my life today.

If you are suffering, ask for help. You don't have to do this alone. Reach out to these people; they can save your life as they have saved mine.

Alcoholics Anonymous: aa.org

Overeaters Anonymous: oa.org

Narcotics Anonymous: na.org

Self-Harm Anonymous: selfharmanonymous.org

Acknowledgments

This book wouldn't exist without the insightful work of my editor, Julia Callahan; thank you for your guidance and honesty. Working with a non-native English writer isn't easy and you helped shape my work with grace and respect. Thank you, Tyson for believing in me and in this book, for seeing the bigger picture; it is an honor to be part of Rare Bird Books. Thank you, Jerry for always being on my side and never giving up on my words, especially when I wanted to quit. Thank you, Phil, Kate, Jim, Jerry, and Anna for your kind words of endorsement, and thank you, Tomas, for your priceless help when I moved to Los Angeles.

Last but not least: Thank you, Benmont, love of my life, husband, and best friend. Thank you for your unconditional love, patience, and inspiration. This novel brings closure to an important chapter of my life. With you, I open a new one, for the next thousand years. I love you.